I0418191

twisted TALES

DARK REFLECTIONS

COPYRIGHT © 2007

LITTLE HEATHENS STUDIO

www.littleheathens.com

STORIES AND WRITING BY

JEREMY HUFF

ARTWORK BY

THOMAS DANIELS

All rights reserved. No part of this book may be used or reproduced in any manner whatsoever without written permission except in the case of brief quotations embodied in critical articles or reviews.

ISBN: 978-0-6151-4669-0

ACKNOWLEDGEMENTS

Jeremy Huff would like to acknowledge the following people for their help and support during the creation of this book:

My wife, Andrea, for her never ending love and support – without her I'd be lost.

To my children, Brayden and Kiefer, for their constant ability to amaze me with their thoughts as well as their actions – they are a constant source of material.

And to my mother, brothers, sister, and friends for their continued support of my writing.

DARK REFLECTIONS

Contents

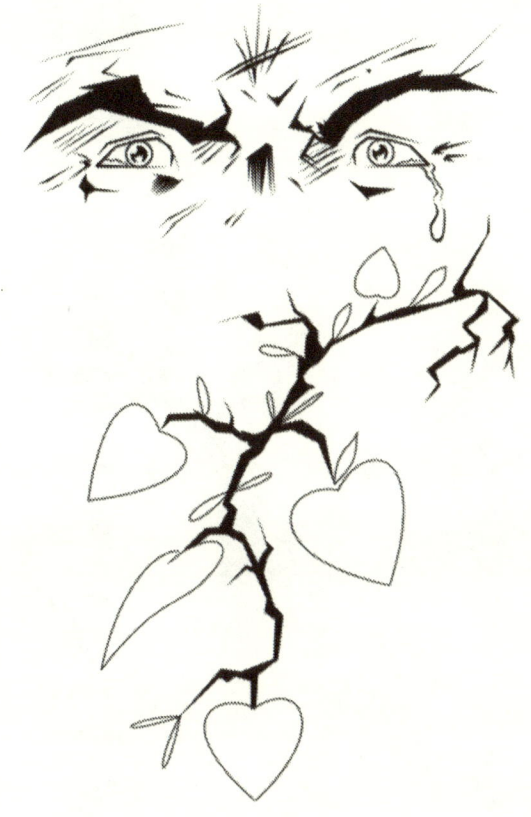

Tattoo Memories

Tattoo Memories

The bell on the glass door, with the very colorful logo of a dragon with raised wings over the words "Forever Inked", rang the presence of a customer. Paul raised the needle from the young man's arm to see who the latest entry was to be. The image that filled his vision was a stereotypical biker: blue jeans covering mammoth legs, faded t-shirt with the Harley-Davidson logo on it stretched to its breaking point by the chest underneath, ratty, sleeveless denim vest, oval shaped sunglasses, and the bandana wrapped around the top of a head very proportional to the rest of the body.

"Help you?" Paul preferred to keep his voice monotone and apathetic. It fit most of his clientele and made it easier to avoid developing friendships.

The biker took a good long look at Paul as if measuring him up for something. He quickly scanned up the blue jeans and the ratty t-shirt, but stopped at Paul's arms. The tattoos that lined both arms seemed to intrigue, or at least entertain, the biker. Evidently satisfied with what he say, he blessed Paul by speaking.

"Need a tat, need it now."

The man's voice was low and guttural staying true to the stereotype. His words weren't that uncommon; hell his looks weren't that uncommon. Inking bikers passing through to some final destination Paul never cared to know made a good portion of Paul's business. Paul had been in the business too long to be flustered by such directness.

"I can take you after I finish this one here. Cool?"

"Hey kid! Give ya 20 bucks to take a walk. You in?"

The young man in the chair almost looked relieved. He got up, grabbed his shirt and looked at Paul. "See you tomorrow?"

Paul nodded. When one of these guys offered a peaceful way out it was wisest to take the lead. The kid took the twenty hanging from the biker's hand and went out the door, his shirt balled in his hand. The biker walked toward the chair, removing his vest and shirt. He sat down heavily in the chair with his back facing Paul.

"I want another one like this one." His finger was attempting to point at a red heart outlined in black. There was a crack that started at the top center and went about half way down giving the heart a split look to it. There were four such hearts on his back, all in a straight row. Each heart contained different letters on top (CY, TR, HM, and EP) and a city name (Culverton, Tulsa, Lawton, and Stihler in order) under the letters.

"Interesting motif you've got going here. What do you want on this one?"

"S and T on top, Shiloh on bottom."

"I don't have a template like these. You wanna go free?" Normally a template was used to create the outline. It gave the tattoo a straight-line quality assuring the proper look and it gave the customer a chance to see an outline of the design before it was permanent. Bikers had a common habit of requesting simple designs without templates. Paul didn't like doing it freehand because there was never a guarantee that it would end up looking just like they wanted, but it was money and he couldn't afford to turn away ready money.

"Yeah man, just freehand it and make it right."

Paul leaned a little closer to study each of the hearts, ready for the familiar stink that seemed to emanate from so many of the bikers. He was pleasantly surprised to find there was no odor except that of soap. A clean biker, wonders never cease. Each heart was very similar, but not perfect. They'd all been done freehand. This guy was always in a hurry to get inked.

"Alright man, you said S and T and Shiloh right?"

The biker just nodded. It suddenly hit Paul. Shiloh was a small city about forty-five miles from his shop; just another insignificant dot on the map. His curiosity peaked and he broke one of his own rules: he asked a question.

"Someone break your heart in Shiloh?"

It was a simple question, truly innocent at heart, but the response was exactly why Paul had made his rule about not asking questions.

"You don't wanna know man."

Knowing the biker was right, but not able to help himself, Paul pushed. "You don't wanna talk about it that's fine, but I'll listen if you wanna talk."

"Your funeral dude. Don't stop while I'm talking and don't fuck it up either. If you're willing to bet your legs on that, I'll tell you."

While losing his legs, or at least the use of them, didn't really appeal to Paul, he still had to know. "No problem. Fire away."

"They call me Heartbreaker cuz I'm responsible for so many broken hearts. I'm not talking about any of that relationship shit either. I break the hearts of people I don't even know man. I'm what you'd call a 'nomad'. I bike all around the country and don't really live anywhere 'cept on my bike. I link up with chicks in all the cities. You'd be surprised how willing most chicks are, 'specially in the small towns, to link up with a biker. Gives 'em a few days away from their boring as shit lives, you know?"

Paul did know. He lived in a small town and had seen many of the locals go off with any biker who happened to drive in. He pulled a sealed needle from the stack and held it up. You had to show the customer you were opening a clean needle, even the bikers wanted to see you open a new one. He pulled out his paint tray and washed it with alcohol, another standard. He then filled three of the cups with ink: black, red, and green. Heartbreaker didn't turn to look at any of these shows of cleanliness. Okay, so not everybody wanted to see you were a clean artist.

"So you get a tat for each woman?"

"You gonna listen or you want me to drop it?" He was frustrated.

"Sorry man, go ahead."

"I told you earlier it wasn't that relationship shit. Besides if I got a tat for each chick I nailed I wouldn't have any room for you to put this one on."

Paul turned the needle on, dipped the tip into the black ink, and started the outline. Heartbreaker didn't even flinch when the needle started cutting through his skin.

"You see, I've got this taste for young meat. A lot of times the young ones are willing enough, they just can't get to me. Parents feed 'em full of shit trying to keep 'em away from me. I don't give up easily though. If I see a piece I want, I sure as fucking God am going to get it. These are all the ones that I wanted that couldn't get to me."

Paul was starting to understand all too well.

"The way I see it, most of the young ones I go after really do want it. I just take it to them. Every once in a while, one of the stupid cunts decides she's gonna tell her daddy or the cops or someone she shouldn't be tellin'. That's when I become a true heartbreaker."

Paul wanted to hear him say the words. He knew what they were going to be, but still wanted to hear them in his own words. He had to be sure this guy was telling the truth before he opened a can of worms he couldn't justify. This guy was evil. Most of Paul's customers were evil, but this guy took the cake. So smug in his abilities that he would sit and tell an absolute stranger the things he did to those little girls. Paul knew he would be leaving town right after he'd been inked and knew the cops didn't have much chance of catching him when he did. After all, how many other people had Heartbreaker told his story too? Paul started to wonder if this guy was going to kill him when he finished the story.

Paul cleaned the needle, dipped it into the red ink, and started coloring the tattoo.

Heartbreaker wasn't giving out any more information, at least not voluntarily. He'd been quiet for the last few minutes and didn't look like he was going to start up again anytime soon. Paul decided not to press it just yet.

Paul's shop was just outside of a small town called Red Hills. The name was obviously derived from some dream the settlers had about it because there were no hills and the ground was yellow. Red Hills had no police force, just the predictable passing by of the state patrol at 11 in the morning and 4 in the afternoon. It was now 3:45 in the afternoon.

Paul cleaned the needle and dipped it into the green ink.

The shop itself was no more than a shanty with a porch that had already fallen most of the way in. A small sign near the highway that read 'TATTOOS' was all that advertised it. Paul averaged one to two customers per day and wouldn't be able to afford the place if he didn't live in the back of it. It hadn't always been this way. Paul once had a nice house in a small city, but that was years ago, before the big change. All of that seemed like a lifetime away now.

Paul cleaned the needle and dipped it into the black ink and started the lettering that would complete the tattoo. Heartbreaker seemed to be sleeping, but Paul wasn't sure or willing to say anything to find out.

A few minutes later, the tattoo was complete and Paul looked at the $3.47 Wal-Mart clock on the wall. It was now 3:58.

"All done 'breaker. Just need to wash it off and have you give it the okay. Oh, and that'll be 80 bucks."

Heartbreaker roused around a little, he had been sleeping after all. He lazily pulled his wallet from his front pocket, via the chain it was clipped to, and pulled out a hundred dollar bill. He laid the bill on the counter and straightened up, stretching and coming back to life.

Paul started wiping off the excess ink with the cleanser in the spray bottle and took another glimpse at the clock: 4:01. State patrol was late today. It fit well into Paul's sense of bad luck lately. Paul kept wiping over the same spot.

"That's good man. Christ, I don't need another fucking bath. Just wipe it down."

Paul took a clean cloth and wiped the now smeared excess ink from the behemoth back. He'd stalled as long as he could. That was all he could do for now.

"You wanna look at it? Make sure it works for you."

"Yeah, where's your mirror?"

Paul pointed to the front wall. There was a full-length mirror propped against the wall. Heartbreaker walked over to it, shirt and vest bundled in one hand. Paul looked at the clock: 4:04. He could feel sweat forming on his brow, helpless to stop it.

His heart pounding so loudly he could hear nothing else, Paul watched as Heartbreaker's long strides covered the short length of the shop. If his calculations were right, Paul would be a dead man in about 4 minute – and Paul was very good at numbers.

As Heartbreaker reached the mirror, a reflection of light flew across the parlor catching his attention. He looked out the glass door just as the state patrol car lazily drove past, the sun reflected perfectly on the recently washed car.

That was all Heartbreaker needed to see. "Looks good man. Keep the change and I'll catch you on the flip side." With that, Heartbreaker walked to the door and watched the patrol car disappear over a small hill. He quickly stepped out the door, down the steps, and got on his motorcycle. Paul walked to the front window and watched him drive off in the opposite direction the state patrol car had gone. Paul grinned.

Heartbreaker didn't have a chance to look in the mirror and see the lovely red rose with green leaves Paul had drawn on. He didn't get to see the letters C.Y. that Paul had put under the rose either. Paul was grateful for the reliable (although it was close today) path the state patrol car took every day. He was grateful for the break he'd been given. Most of all, he was grateful to God for giving him this opportunity.

Along with the true look of his latest tattoo, there were other things Heartbreaker didn't know. He didn't know the tattoos on Paul Young's arms were temporary, painstakingly put on every three days to keep the image believable. He didn't know Paul used to be a happily married, biological engineer in the nearby city of Culverton. He didn't know that Paul had quit his job after his fifteen-year old daughter, Christy, had been raped and killed by a drifter who'd never been found. He didn't know Paul couldn't take the loss and eventually drove his wife, and everyone else in his life, away. He didn't know Paul had lost his job as he spent countless weeks tracking the killer of his daughter to a tattoo shop that only remembered one thing about the man; he had gotten a tattoo of a broken heart. He didn't know Paul had been looking forward to this day for many years.

He also didn't know the one thing that he would soon wish he did. Paul had taken something with him before his career as a biological engineer had been cut short, something deadly. He didn't know Paul had placed this deadly something into the green ink. Most of all, he didn't know that this deadly something was pumping through his veins as he drove down the highway on his Harley-Davidson motorcycle. He didn't know that soon all of his internal organs would begin to liquefy leaving him immobile for the remaining three days of his pain filled life.

Paul's grin widened. He reached out and flipped the 'Yes We're Open' sign over to 'Sorry Closed'. Then Paul Young went to pack his few things before heading back to Culverton, back to life.

Good Samaritan

Good Samaritan

John was filling his truck and happened to be the first person to see the figure coming toward the station. He silently wondered who would be walking around in the heat of mid July. The pump handle clicked and John looked down out of habit. He quickly reset the automatic lock on the pump. When he looked up again, he could see the person walking toward him was a man. He could also tell the man was a stranger. Strangers didn't come into Browning very often and the citizens preferred it that way.

Gwen's little gas station sat on the highway two miles from town and saw several travelers a day, but never a walking one. The handle popped, but John kept his eyes on the stranger this time. The man reached the gas station's driveway giving John his first good look.

The stranger stood about six feet tall and looked rather puny to John. He was dressed in dusty blue jeans, a plain white t-shirt, and a denim jacket. He walked with his chin against his chest and took long strides for his height. John guessed him to be in his late teens or early twenties.

Seeming to feel John's gaze on him, the stranger looked up and toward him. John held eye contact and the stranger nodded his head in a rural wave. John nodded back. The man walked through the glass door of the station and disappeared behind the barrage of cigarette ads.

Not liking the idea of Gwen being alone in the station with a stranger, John quickly rounded the gauge to the next dollar and capped his tank. Holding back the urge to run, John slowly walked to the front door. When he reached the door he could see the stranger talking to Gwen at the counter. It didn't look like she was nervous and John took an extra second to regain his composure. There was no reason to overreact and get everybody worried for nothing.

He pushed open the door and walked up to the counter. The stranger took a step to the side to make more room and John relaxed further. This kid was jittery and nervous, not intimidating in the least. John gave Gwen the same smile he'd been giving her for the last eight years and she returned the gesture.

John took a short glance to capture all of Gwen's features once again. Her curly red hair, now with random streaks of gray, flowed down to her shoulders where it contrasted beautifully with her blue smock. At just under five and a half feet tall, her figure was cut in half by the counter giving him a very nice few of her ample breasts. The smock did its best to cover up the resulting cleavage, but John knew when to look to defeat the defense.

He realized he was staring at her hypnotizing hazel eyes and spoke to break the spell.

"How's it goin' Gwen?"

"Doin' pretty good John. You?"

"Can't complain."

John looked back to the stranger and nodded again. The man turned his gaze to the floor as Gwen took the cue to introduce him.

"This here is Rob. Says his car ran out of gas a few miles up the road. Ain't that right Rob?"

The stranger mumbled a yes, but didn't look at John. John looked at Gwen and raised an eyebrow. Gwen shrugged her shoulders and rang up his gas.

"Coffee today hon?"

"Yeah, thanks. So Rob, you got a gas can with ya?"

The man finally met John's eyes and shook his head. When he spoke, his voice was deeper than John had imagined and John wondered if he'd guessed the stranger too young.

"Nope. And I don't have much money either. I was trying to work something out with Gwen here."

A smile (devious if you asked John) crept across his face when he said her name. Not liking the way the stranger looked or sounded, John decided he would offer a solution to get the man out of Browning as quickly as possible.

"Well, I'll tell you what. I got a full can and I don't need to be anywhere for a little while. How'd you feel about me giving you a ride back to your car?"

The smile quickly disappeared, but was immediately replaced with a smaller, friendlier one. John fought off the smile that was trying to creep over his lips. He'd successfully thwarted the young man's plan, whatever it had been.

"I guess that'd be fine. I'm sorry I can't pay you anything for your trouble."

"That's okay. Just consider it a good Samaritan act."

"That's very kind of you. I'd appreciate it."

"Sure thing. Just let me get my coffee and we'll be on our way."

John walked to the coffee counter and realized he'd forgotten to get his mug in his haste. He quickly pulled a Styrofoam cup from the dispenser, filled it up, capped it, and walked back to the counter.

"Losin' your mind there John?"

He gave her the warmest smile he could and pulled out his money.

"Guess so. Forgot my mug at home today."

"Don't think I've ever seen you forget that before."

"Yeah, doesn't happen very often."

He turned to the stranger, who hadn't moved from his original spot.

"You ready to head out Rob?"

The stranger nodded and turned back to Gwen.

"Thanks for all the help Gwen. You have very nice people in this town."

Gwen gave an awkward smile and handed John his change. John smiled back and felt a sudden protective urge towards Gwen. This man was making her nervous and John had to make it stop.

"Come on young man. Let's get moving."

His voice contained a tone of anger and Gwen looked at him in shock. He immediately regretted his tone, but decided to ignore it for the moment.

John turned and walked out the door, the stranger just a few steps behind him. John gave a last look at Gwen to be sure she was okay and was comforted to see her smile at him.

The two men made their way across the short gap between the station and John's truck. John walked to the driver's side door and climbed in without acknowledging the stranger. The stranger stood by the passenger door and looked around shyly. John honked the horn and the stranger jumped. John laughed and waved for the man to get into the truck. The man quickly opened the door and climbed onto the seat, staying as far from John as possible.

John waved to Gwen as he pulled out of the station's lot and on to the highway. Gwen waved back and John felt his heart speed up a little.

"So, your name is Rob. Is that short for Robert?"

The man just shook his head. The stranger had been quiet in the station, but now he wasn't talking at all.

"Where's your car at?"

He looked out the window and pointed towards a hill several miles away.

"Just on the other side of that hill."

The more he rode with the stranger, the better he felt about getting him away from Gwen. There was something strange about this guy, but he couldn't put his finger on it just yet. He decided to try to get a little more information out of him.

"What brings you to Browning?"

"Nothing. Just driving through and ran out of gas."

He answered this question very quickly and it unnerved John even more.

"Where are you heading then?"

The man finally turned to face John.

"I'm heading from Detroit to college in Buffalo. Thought I'd take the long way around and see some of the country. You know?"

He'd been right about the age after all. This was just a punk kid who'd run out of gas. He relaxed and thought about the feelings he'd had earlier about Gwen. He decided he would finally ask Gwen out for coffee. After all, he'd been thinking about it for years now.

"That's my car. Right there."

John had been so involved in his introspection he'd driven past the car. He pulled to the shoulder and reversed to within a few feet of the Toyota Celica's trunk.

"Nice car."

"Thanks."

The stranger didn't wait for a cue this time. He jumped out of the truck and walked to his car. John checked for any passing cars, not a real threat on this stretch of road, and got out as well. He walked to the rear of the truck and opened the tailgate. He always kept a full tank of gas tied to the bed of the truck for farm use. He was about to climb into the truck when he noticed the two vehicles were back to back.

"Hey kid. If I give you a couple of gallons, is that going to be enough to get you somewhere else?"

No answer, again. He turned to see what the stranger was doing and was met by a fast moving object as it struck his head. The force of the blow blurred his vision and knocked him off balance. He fell against the tailgate and struggled to keep his feet under him. The stranger grabbed him below the waist and threw him, head over heels, into the bed of the truck before John could react.

Lying on his back, he could see the stranger standing over him.

"Yep. Browning sure is a nice town."

The man kicked John in the head and John thought he was going to pass out, but his vision focused after a few seconds. The stranger untied the gas can from the bed of the truck and removed the cap. John struggled to organize everything that was happening in his mind. He tried to ask Rob questions, but heard only mumbling nonsense come from his mouth. The man began pouring gasoline over John's legs and waist.

The coldness of the liquid shocked John's system and he was finally able to speak.

"What are you doing?"

The stranger stopped and gave John a look of dumbfounded awe and then began laughing hysterically.

"You backwoods hillbillies man. You crack me up. I'm killing you. What am I doing? That's rich."

He continued laughing as he poured more gas on John's stomach and chest.

"Why?"

He didn't stop pouring this time. Instead, he emptied the gas on John's face, threw the can to the side of the road, and moved to the tailgate before answering.

"Why? Why is there always a why?"

John tried to say something, but the fuel was burning his eyes and taking the oxygen out of his lungs. He began coughing and tried to spit the liquid out.

"It was a rhetorical question dumbass. That means you're not supposed to answer it. Besides, you'll find that opening your mouth for very long at all is going to be very painful. I've seen people pass out just from trying. It ain't pretty! Looking all pitiful and guppying for air like that. Downright pathetic if you ask me."

The man reached into his jacket pocket and pulled out a book of matches. He struck the first one and threw it at John. It blew out before it left his hand and fell harmlessly on John's leg.

"I saw the way you were playing with that woman in the gas station man. I think I'll give her a little visit after we're done here. You know, just to make sure she's okay and all. What do you think about that?"

"Doan ya fck…"

He couldn't finish the words because of the excruciating pain in his throat, but he wasn't going to let that stop him. He kicked at the stranger and felt brief satisfaction when he connected.

"Very brave John. You've got more energy than I gave you credit for, but I'm boring of this little game and it's time I move on. However, before I leave you, I'd like to ask you a question. Don't worry, I don't expect you to answer. Didn't you notice the car is facing the wrong direction? That should have clued you off that something was up, but you've got your dick pointing towards that good looking old lady at the station. Look where that got you."

He kicked John in the groin and laughed. John coughed up a mouthful of coppery tasting bile, but couldn't get his body to double over. The stranger jumped out of the bed of the truck and walked to the passenger side in direct line of John's sight. He lit another match and threw it at John, but it blew out and fell harmlessly next to the previous one.

"If it makes you feel any better John, there's nothing personal here. You just happened to be here when I was looking for someone. A few minutes later and it may have been your girlfriend back there. Doesn't really matter to me. Say good night."

He pulled another single match out and lit it, but this time he lit the rest of the book with the burning match. The flame glowed bright and high in the stranger's hand as it reflected in the pupils of John's eyes. John struggled to move, but his body denied him anything useful. Instead, a few twitches and kicks were his only rewards.

The stranger flicked the brightly burning matchbook at him and it didn't extinguish this time. The gas erupted into flames and John's mouth opened in a mock scream, unable to even make a sound.

The flames instantly engulfed John's legs and body and quickly spread up his chest and face. He began to feel the burning of his flesh and struggled more fiercely to get his body to respond, but nothing worked. By the time he regained any control of his voice there was no air left to produce a noise.

Rob drove past the gas station and waved to Gwen as she cleaned the pumps. She smiled and waved back, oblivious of the thin line of black smoke rising over the hill behind her. As she watched the Toyota Celica drive away she wondered if John would finally ask her out for dinner.

A Modern Romance

A Modern Romance

He loved her and she loved him. He never doubted her love for him despite the occasional questionable actions she performed. Sometimes when they were in public she would just walk next to him acting like she didn't even know who he was. That pissed him off. However, she would always make up for it in some small way or another. He could put up with her cold shoulder attitude in public; the private times more than made up for them anyway.

There was nothing he loved more than to sit alone with her. They would sit together for hours, never saying a word. Sometimes the television was on, sometimes the radio, and sometimes there was no noise at all and they just enjoyed the company of each other. Those were the nights he liked the best. He would watch her fall asleep in her bedroom then would leave quietly so as to not wake her. It was the little things like that that made their relationship work as well as it did.

The first time he saw her he knew they were destined to be together forever. He was buying a paper at a corner newsstand when she came up and bought a magazine. Her voice forced him to look around to see who was making such an angelic sound. His eyes fell upon the most beautiful woman he'd ever seen in his life, movies and magazines included. He'd been too awed to speak to her and by the time he'd regained his composure she was already gone. For the next two weeks, Terrence had returned to the same newsstand in the hopes of finding her. His hopes went unfulfilled.

Fate struck again nearly six months after their first encounter. He'd given up any hopes of seeing her again months before and was startled when he bumped into her in the convenience store next to his office building. He'd just purchased a paper and was looking at the front page news as he walked toward the door. She had turned the corner of one of the aisles (Terrence could not remember which aisle for the life of him) and they had come face to face. Again stunned by her beauty he stood looking in awe at her. She'd apologized and went to go around him when his senses returned and he broke the ice.

She told him her name was Sharon and he fell in love instantly. The conversation lasted no more than a minute, but it was long enough for Terrence to find out where she worked. The name of the bank she worked at was etched permanently into his memory.

Just like that his life had changed. To be closer to her he quickly changed banks. He had no idea what she did at the bank, but he silently hoped she was a teller and he would be able to make their meetings seem accidental. Nature never works so easily though. She turned out to be a bookkeeper of some sort who stayed in the back of the bank. Always near and just out of sight.

He'd been a little depressed the day he found out they wouldn't "accidentally" meet through his banking plot, but the depression only lasted as long as his next trip to the bank. She'd been leaving for lunch, a little late for some reason, and they had passed each other in the lobby. She gave him a nice smile (one he has since learned is her honest smile) on her way out.

From that day forward Terrence went to lunch fifteen minutes earlier than he usual. His lunch path always included the bank before noon in the hopes of catching a glimpse of her as she went to lunch. Some days he was lucky, others he would spend the entire lunch hour waiting in vain. The payoff was worth the gamble in his mind.

The rest was, as they say, history. The relationship somehow transgressed into what they had now. He always made a point of trying not to smother her with attention and his presence. Occasionally, he would not come to her house and let her have some time to herself. Relationships are funny that way. No matter how much you love someone you still need your own time and Terrence respected that. It pained him not to see her, but he didn't want to ruin the relationship.

As he watched, her eyes begin to get too heavy for her to keep them raised and he was struck with so much love he almost began to cry. How could he have lived his life before meeting her? What purpose had his life contained before her? He could come up with no answer for either question. She had given him reason and purpose in his life. He owed her his everything.

Headlights ran across the window startling him with their blinding brightness. He looked to see if the car would pull into the driveway. His heart began beating quicker and he could feel his face beginning to flush.

Who the hell would be stopping by at this hour?

The car continued past the house. His heart and temperature began to return to normal. It was no one for Sharon after all.

One night, early in their relationship, Terrence had not planned on going over to her house. He was going to work at his home that night and decided to make it one of her "alone" nights. When he finished early he'd changed his mind and drove to her neighborhood anyway. When he walked up to her driveway he was taken aback by the added car in it. His first thoughts were of family members or co-workers. Maybe he'd get to meet some of the people in her life tonight.

His thoughts of an innocent encounter were quickly broken. He'd looked through the window to see where she was when he saw her kissing another man on her couch. Fury filled him. He wanted to break down the door and beat the other man to death. On the one night he decided not to show up, she'd made another date and was now kissing him right in front of Terrence.

Fighting every fiber of his body he'd walked quietly away that night. He'd have to let it go and see what her true intentions were for the both of them.

The man had never been a problem again. Terrence knew that she wasn't really in love with the other guy, but kept his mouth shut because in the end he had won the battle. He kept telling himself that he had to move beyond the one occurrence and start to trust her again, but his mind would still question her faithfulness at certain times.

Another set of headlights washed across the window startling him out of his waking dream and drawing his eyes away from Sharon. She was sleeping now and her beauty was cherubic. In the nine months since their first meeting she'd only grown more beautiful in his eyes.

The headlights did not continue past her house this time. A car was pulling into her driveway and someone was getting out. Terrence's heart began beating too quickly again. He looked at his watch. Eleven thirty. On a Tuesday night, that was too late for a family member to come over. It had to be someone else. Someone who didn't know he was here.

A man, dressed in blue jeans and a polo shirt, walked up the walkway and rang the bell. Sharon was startled from her sleep and ran to the door before Terrence could respond. She opened the door and the man bent down and kissed her - with Terrence standing right there! She didn't pull away or tell him to stop or anything to spare Terrence's feelings. Terrence couldn't stand it any longer. He had to confront her on this while he had the anger and the guts.

Terrence walked to the front door and stood behind the stranger debating which words to use. Before he could come up with something suitable for such an atrocity, Sharon saw him and he had to react quickly. Terrence pulled his keys from his pocket gripping the oversized Toyota key's base in his palm. The remainder of the key protruded between his index and middle finger. While he was removing and adjusting his keys, the man had turned in the doorway and was now facing Terrence.

Before even realizing what he was doing, Terrence felt his fist moving towards the man's neck. The tip of the key hesitated briefly against his neck as rounded metal met skin, but the pressure being applied by Terrence forced it through. Terrence was surprised at how little blood was released by the key and by how quiet the man was being. The surprise washed away when he pulled the key out and a geyser erupted from the man's neck. Still, the man stayed quiet as Terrence watched him fall first to his knees then on his face. Terrence had a brief respect for the man's ability to remain silent through so much obvious pain.

Sharon's scream brought his gaze back to his beloved.

"What's wrong with you Sharon?"

She didn't answer him with words. Instead she started backing away from the door and further into her house. Terrence followed at the same pace.

"I trusted you Sharon. I love you with all my heart and this is how you repay me?"

Sharon's back was against a wall now and her eyes were darting in all directions. Terrence was now no more than two feet away and still moving toward her. Her mind was racing, trying to make sense of it all. She asked the only thing she could think of.

"Who are you?"

Terrence stopped his approach and looked at her quizzically. How could she not know him? They'd met at the newsstand, in the store, and he banked at her bank. She had to know him; they were in love.

"It's me, your boyfriend, Terrence. We're in love. We were going to be married someday."

"I don't know you. Scott is my boyfriend." Her arm stiffened as she pointed to the body lying in the doorway.

"No, he's not! He was trying to take you away from me, just like the other guy. But neither one of them can ever take you away from me. We're destined to be together. It's fate. Love has found a way."

Sharon looked blankly at him. She decided to take her chances and run rather than wait for this lunatic to grab her. As she turned to run, his arm shot out and grabbed her by the collar of her shirt. The sudden jerk on her head caused her to lose her balance and she fell to the floor. Terrence was on top of her before she was even aware she'd fallen.

"He took you didn't he? We were in love and he took you away. That can't be, we are destined to live together. To die together." His eyes came alive with the last statement.

His weight on her was squeezing the air out, forcing Sharon to gasp for each breath. His hands wrapped around her throat and tightened. Her face turned from red to blue as the oxygen was blocked from her lungs. She was flailing her arms and legs trying for some foothold to push the weight off of her. She failed.

He stayed in that position for several minutes after she quit fighting him. He'd just killed the one love of his life. He went into the kitchen and retrieved a knife sizable enough for the task then came back into the entrance way and sat down next to Sharon. What was the point of a loveless life anyway? He could come up with no good answer and decided he had been right in the words he spoke to her. They were destined to die together.

A Cry For Help

Jack Romero was heading home after a quiet dinner and a few drinks at his favorite Italian restaurant when he heard the cry. At first he thought the voice was coming from one of the buildings along the street, but they were all dark and it was too late for any tourists to be in this area. Jack liked to take this path on weeknights because of that solitude. The voice sounded like that of a child, but had an echoing effect that was causing Jack trouble. In such a wide-open area of buildings he couldn't tell where an echo could be generated.

At the restaurant he'd had a couple glasses of wine, but he was sure that hadn't been enough to cause him to hear sounds. Beginning to question himself, he resumed his walk. The tiny voice called out its one word cry again.

"Help!"

The voice was full of anxiety and fear this time and Jack was sure he wasn't hearing things. The echo effect had toned down and he thought the sound was coming from below him. He dropped to his knees and put his head to the ground.

"Help!"

Having his ear pressed to the ground didn't make the voice any clearer than before. The idea that putting your head to the ground to hear things only worked when the object was large enough to vibrate the ground suddenly hit him. He stayed on his knees but took his head off the ground.

He decided he should try to get the person's attention.

"Hello? Is there someone out here?"

There was no answer and Jack was still unable to determine where the voice had come from. He began crawling around the sidewalk with his head close to the ground.

"Help!"

The voice was louder this time and Jack was sure it was coming from below him.

How the hell does a voice come from below me when I'm standing on a freaking sidewalk?

He sat on his knees pondering the question and wondering if the alcohol had done more damage than he'd thought. Would the answer have come quicker if he'd just passed on one of the glasses?

Why am I thinking about this shit now? There's somebody, probably a child, calling for help and I'm pondering why I'm so slow in coming up with an answer.

Something wet touched his cheek taking his mind away from the internal struggle. He looked up to the sky that had been threatening rain since he'd left the restaurant. Another drop hit him on the other cheek. Then another landed on his forehead. The sky opened up and released one of those surprise downpours Florida was famous for.

The sound of the rain pounding against the pavement and his face drowned out all other noises and the cry for help was momentarily forgotten. Jack's custom designed suit was becoming drenched and he could feel his undershirt sticking to his skin. The rain was coming down quicker than the typical downpour and small rivulets were beginning to form in the streets. The water ran along the curb and down the gutter where it splashed into quickly forming ponds below.

The sound of the water dropping into the gutter produced a splashing sound with an echo effect. The sound reminded Jack of something that he couldn't quite put his finger on. The rivulets changed into tiny streams that began pulling some of the trash in the street to the gutter. The connection dawned on Jack and he felt like slapping his forehead in disgust.

He dropped his one hundred and eighty-five pound, six foot two frame flat against the sidewalk, belly first, and draped his head over the curb. He then began scooting along the curb until he came to the gutter grating. There were a few pieces of paper that had gotten stuck in the grate. He pulled them out and threw them on the sidewalk behind him.

Even after placing his face against the curb and squinting his eyes he was unable to tell if somebody was in there. He changed his tactic and turned his head so his ear was facing the grate opening.

"Help!"

The voice was louder and edgier now. Whoever was down there was beginning to panic. In this position Jack could tell the voice was a child's. He couldn't tell how old, but he guessed a kid still in elementary school. He turned his head so his eyes were once again facing the opening and looked for the source of the voice. It was no use. The opening was too dark or too deep to see anything.

He reached into the inside pocket of his jacket and pulled out his Zippo. He'd tried to quit smoking a few times over the years, but the compulsion was too strong and he'd lost all the battles. It wasn't so much that he wanted to quit, but working in the accounting office at City Hall did have its disadvantages. It had occurred to Jack more than once that quitting his job would be easier than quitting smoking. He felt a small sense of victory as he lowered his hand, lighter in grasp, into the gutter.

Smoking may kill me, but it may save this kid's life too. Think they'll take that into consideration the next time they pass a No Smoking Law? Oh no! We have to point out the negatives, never the positives.

A small grin formed on his lips. Using the skill and agility that only a twelve year smoking veteran was capable of, Jack opened the cover of the lighter and spun the flint. He'd splurged for the limited edition Zippo about four years ago when he'd been given a promotion at work. He'd always thought there was nothing more annoying than a lighter that wouldn't stay lit long enough to light a cigarette. He was proven wrong when they came out with those damn child safety locks on the disposable lighters. Zippo is a brand for smokers who want an easy and reliable lighter. It was one of the few purchases he'd ever made without questioning it later.

The flame roared to life illuminating the chamber below the grate. He began searching the chamber for the child. Jack could see small pieces of trash stuck to the walls and small rocks lining the floor, but no child.

"Help!"

The voice was coming from directly below him. The child was leaning against the wall just out of his sight.

"I'm here kid. I'm going to try to get you out, but you have to stay calm and help me. Okay?"

"Help! The water is getting deeper."

Jack sat up and looked around for some sign of life that he'd missed earlier. He wasn't sure he'd be able to help this kid by himself. It looked hopeless; there was no life to be seen. He was alone and he would have to find a way to save the boy's life one way or another.

Jack, still on his knees, reached down and tried to pull the grating up. It didn't budge.

How the hell did that little bastard get down there in first place?

He looked around for some sort of tool he could use to pry the grate open. His eyes landed on what looked like a small bar. It was glittering in the rain and Jack guessed it was made out of metal. He reached over to grab it. When he pulled up on the bar it moved about two inches before locking and

Jack almost fell forward with the sudden lack of motion. He crawled closer and saw it was attached to a manhole cover.

Jack felt like smacking his forehead again in disgust, but thought better of it. He stood up and straddled the cover with his legs spread. He bent down and grabbed the handle preparing himself for the task. Mustering as much strength as he could, he jerked on the bar. The ease of which it moved surprised him and he fell backwards, dragging the cover across the sidewalk as he went. He landed in a little puddle with his legs spread open and the cover in between them.

Recovering from the surprise fall, he noticed the cover was off the hole and he had access to the kid stuck below. A rush of adrenaline kicked in and he crawled to the opening. He stuck his head in the hole while re-igniting the lighter.

"I got ya kid. Can you climb over to the hole and get out?"

The entire chamber was visible this time and he could see the boy standing in the corner. The boy was older than Jack had thought. He looked to be about thirteen. He was dressed in an oversized sports jacket (Jack couldn't see the logo), baggy pants, and a stocking cap. Jack would have wondered why the kid was wearing a stocking cap in mid-September if he had the time.

The boy stepped away from the wall a few steps and Jack noticed the water wasn't building up at all. The water was going around the platform the boy was standing on and down into a deeper gutter. Jack opened his mouth to ask him if this was some kind of joke, but the words never came out.

The boy reached into his jacket pocket and pulled out something that reflected the light from the lighter. It took Jack a second to register what it was. Jack was never a gun enthusiast so he didn't know the gun was a 9mm pistol. He was a city worker, however, and he did know that it was a gun and that all guns are capable of killing. His mind began screaming at his body to move out of the way, but his body seemed to be ignoring him.

The kid pointed the gun directly at Jack and pulled the trigger. Jack's eyes registered a smile across the boy's face as the explosion of firing pin on powder filled his ears. His mind was still yelling at his body to run away and his body was still not listening. He had no idea the bullet had already passed through his throat leaving a rather clean exit hole for a 9mm wound. His head dropped and dangled over the edge of the hole. Thankfully, he was not able to see his own blood turning the rivulets he'd witnessed earlier a crimson color.

Jack's eyes were looking the only place they could, directly in front of him. The boy climbed up the metal rungs lining the sewer wall and hoisted himself out of the hole. As he passed, Jack heard him build up a mouth full of phlegm and spit it. Jack knew the boy had just spit on him, but he did not feel it hit.

"Thanks for the help mutha fucka."

Jack heard laughter; too much laughter to be created from just the one kid. He heard other voices begin talking, but was unable to turn his head to see who was there. He knew it was nobody that was going to help him and he prayed for death.

"Nice job T! Popped a fuckin' cap right in the mutha fucka's throat man!"

"Damn straight! Told you I could do it Dawg."

"You shoulda seen the dumbass lookin' for ya when you was yellin' for help. It was funnier than shit, yo!"

"Now tag the mutha fucka and let's get out of here."

Jack heard a sound that reminded him of a penny shaking around in a soda can. It wasn't until he heard the hiss of the spray can that he understood what tagging meant. Jack's vision went black and he died listening to the hiss of paint from an aerosol can. Jack silently thanked God for letting him off easy.

RAVE ON

Rave On

Pounding. More pounding. Sheryl wanted to close her eyes, but she still had no control. She'd lost all track of time long ago and was glad for it now. Her torture continued and she was forced to watch it as it unfolded before her.

She knew the first. It was Michael and she had come to the party with him. The girl who'd come up next had been Sheryl's friend at one time, but that seemed like a lifetime ago. The third one looked familiar, but she couldn't be sure. The rest of the faces, she'd stopped counting after the sixth, blended together into a single anonymous being.

Sheryl thought herself away from what was happening and her mind took her back to an earlier argument with her mother.

"I know what goes on at those parties. They're dangerous."

Her mother had found the rave poster in her room while Sheryl was in school. Sheryl had plans to meet Jenny at eight, but her mom had stopped her on her way out. Sheryl could tell this was going to be one of those hairy types of arguments by her mother's tone.

"They're not dangerous. Just because they report something on 60 Minutes doesn't make it true."

Her mother waved the poster in front of her face.

"There are all kinds of drugs at these things. Crazy kids hopped up on who knows what. I don't want you going."

"I'm going with some friends. We watch out for each other. We just like to listen to the music and dance. Not all teenagers are whacked out drug freaks."

"I'm not worried about you. I'm worried about somebody doing something to you. You're only fifteen years old for God's sake."

"Oh please mother. I think I can watch out for myself. Give me some credit."

A look of anguish covered her mother's face and Sheryl felt bad for using that tone, but it was the only way to get her point across.

"If you want to be popular, there's other ways of doing it you know."

Sheryl couldn't keep a slight laugh from escaping her.

"If I wanted to be popular I would have just become a cheerleader like you."

She'd hurt her mother and she knew it. The look on her face said it all, but it was too late to worry about that now.

"You are not going! Do you understand me?"

She stared into her mother's eyes, judging just how far she could push. Her mom was already at the breaking point and she knew it: time for plan B.

"Fine! You win, as usual. Can Jenny still stay the night at least?"

She knew the words that would get to her mother the most and she emphasized them well. It was a trick that had taken her months to learn and years to perfect, but when she did it right it was well worth it.

Her mother's face softened and a little smile crept across her face. She knew Sheryl's games and she knew when she'd won.

"Sure. But don't think for a second that I'm going to let you all go out."

"Fine. We'll just sit up in my room and watch TV all night."

"Good. You can order pizza if you want and I'll take you to rent a movie. That should be plenty for you to do."

Sheryl turned and ran up the stairs to her room, making a point to slam the door for good measure. Her mom, satisfied she'd won, sat on the couch with a victory smile pasted to her face.

In her room, Sheryl called Jenny.

"Hey, my mom found the flyer."

"Oh shit. Now what're you going to do?"

"It's all worked out. Come on over and we'll head out."

"She's gonna let you go?"

"Of course not. She blew a fucking gasket, but when have we ever let that stop us?"

"So how're we gonna go?"

"I told you, I've got it figured out. My mom wants to buy us pizza and a movie like we're a couple of goddamned kids."

"Gawd. Parents are so stupid sometimes. Hey, if I come over you better have a way to get to that rave. If I miss it I'm gonna be pissed at you forever."

"Don't worry about it. Have I ever let you down?"

"I'm on my way. See you in ten."

Someone strapped another mask on her face bringing her out of her daydream. A new face hovered above her. She didn't recognize this guy either. He mumbled something in her ear, but she couldn't hear any better than she could move. She had no idea what he was saying, but she was sure it had to be something she didn't want to hear anyway.

His body began moving and she could tell the pounding had continued. She pushed herself away from it again.

A box of pizza crusts and several empty cans of soda sat on the floor in front of the couch. Sheryl and Jenny sat on the floor next to it while Sheryl's mom slept on the couch. The movie they'd rented, a slow romance Sheryl had purposely chosen, neared its completion on the television in front of them.

Sheryl turned to Jenny and smiled. Jenny nodded her approval back. Sheryl reached up to her mom and shook her shoulder.

"Mom, the show's over. You should go to bed."

Her mother opened her eyes and tried to focus on the clock.

"What time is it?"

"It's about 11:30. We're going to go to my room and talk for a little while, but we'll be quiet so you can sleep."

"Alright. Shut off all the lights and the TV on your way up. I'm gonna go ahead and hit the hay."

"Alright mom. Good night."

"Night hon. I'm sorry I yelled at you earlier, but I just want you to be safe."

"I know mom. It's okay."

Her mother sat up and walked up the stairs to her bedroom. Jenny waited until she was out of hearing range.

"What was that all about?"

"Since my dad died she tries not to make me mad for some reason. Anytime we have a fight she feels the need to apologize."

"Wow. I wish my mom and dad would do that with me."

"Trust me. It gets very old, very quick. You don't want it."

"Whatever. Are we gonna go now?"

"Not yet. She's going to wait until the lights are out and she hears my door close. I know her."

Sheryl shut off the television and all of the lights on the ground floor. The two of them walked up the steps and into Sheryl's room. Sheryl shut off the light and turned on a lamp.

"How long do we have to wait?"

"Not long. Maybe ten minutes."

"What's the deal with the lamp?"

"She'll open her door and check to make sure a light is on. If we went straight to bed she'd be in here in a heartbeat. She doesn't really trust me even though she says she does."

"I know the feeling."

A few minutes later they heard her mother's door creak open. A few seconds after that they heard it close again. Sheryl looked at Jenny and gave her a wicked smile.

"Showtime."

The mask had been removed. The crowd that she'd seen all night long had diminished greatly. Where a crowd of fifteen to twenty people had stood all night long, now three or four people stood. She felt hope rise in her chest, but it quickly disappeared when someone strapped another mask on. Another mask, another face. Sheryl ran away again.

They'd made it all the way out of Sheryl's house without her mother noticing. When they got to the end of the block, Jenny used her cellular phone to call Michael.

"Pick us up at the gas station by Sher's house…yeah now."

"Where is he?"

"At the rave. Said he'll be there in about fifteen."

"Excellent. That'll give us some time to pick up some supplies."

They looked at each other and laughed.

At the gas station they bought a couple of sodas, four chocolate bars, and a can of lighter fluid. Michael drove up in his Ford Explorer a few minutes later and they headed to the rave.

Michael was full of energy and started talking as soon he saw them.

"Did you all get your supplies?"

Jenny held up the bag and shook it.

"Excellent babes. Let the party begin."

The guy crawled off of her, but the mask remained strapped to her face. She couldn't see anyone in the crowd anymore, but refused to let her hopes rise this time. Nobody else climbed on her. She floated off once again.

The rave was full on by the time they arrived. It was being held in and around an old airplane hangar and people were strewn everywhere. Sheryl recognized a few of them, but the majority of them were unknowns. Barry, a school friend, came out of the car Michael had parked next to.

"Hey ladies. Got your supplies?"

Jenny grabbed the bag out of the Explorer and held it up for Barry's inspection.

"Good job girls. Got your sugars for afterward, but the fluid's no good here. There's a Huffer down by the hangar that'll set you up, but if you want some good shit talk to the dude with the paint masks."

"We don't want anything that's gonna kill us Bare. What is it anyway?"

Jenny jumped in before Barry could respond.

"Sher, don't be such a dweeb. If Bare says it's good shit, it's good shit."

Michael stepped around the Explorer and tapped Barry's fist with his own.

"Yeah Sheryl, chill. Where's this dude at Bare?"

Barry pointed to one of the trashcan fires burning to the side of the hangar. All three of them followed his finger and saw the largest group of people was surrounding the trashcan.

Michael spoke, "Must be a popular man. Looks like he's got the whole party at his post."

"Told you dude. You wanna be at this party, you gotta talk to that dude. Now, if you'll excuse me, I've got a little party of my own to get back to."

Barry saluted Michael and then climbed back into the car he'd just exited. Sheryl could see a girl she didn't recognize in the car when Barry opened the door. She had a painters mask on her head and her eyes were closed. Michael and Jenny obviously saw the same thing because they both started laughing.

Sheryl took her opening, "Looked like she was kind of out of it. She deserves Barry and all that involves."

The three of them made their way to the trashcan and stood in the surprisingly straight line. There were groups of people broken off to all directions of the line. Most of them had painting masks on top of their heads. Sheryl watched a guy as he pulled the mask over his face. His eyes closed and he began to waver on his feet. A girl standing next to him pulled the mask off his face and put it back on top of his head. The guy dropped to his knees and then dropped back on his butt.

Michael tapped her on her shoulder.

"Looks like some good shit doesn't it?"

Sheryl nodded absently.

They got to the front of the line and were greeted by an older white guy wearing baggy clothes and a stocking cap. Behind him sat a truck with several other guys sitting on the tailgate. The bed of the truck was full of spray cans and painting masks.

His voice was deep and rough. "Welcome to the party. What can I do for you?"

Sheryl was the first in line.

"I don't know. What's this gonna cost me?"

"Masks are two bucks, sprays are five."

"What is it?"

A grim smile crept across his lips.

"That's a trade secret my dear. Now, do you want one or not? You're holding up the line."

Sheryl hesitated. The man leaned closer to her and whispered.

"I'll tell you what. You're a cute girl. I'll make you a deal. You buy a spray and I'll give you the mask. Whatdya say?"

She smiled at him. "Okay, thanks."

The man turned to the guys in the truck and held up the index finger on both of his hands. One of the guys grabbed a mask and handed it to the other one. That guy sprayed a mist into the mask and handed it to the man in front.

"Five bucks pretty."

Sheryl handed him a five-dollar bill and took the mask. Michael followed her and gave the man seven dollars for a sprayed mask. Jenny walked past the trashcan and the man. They regrouped next to several dozen people at the edge of the fire's light. Sheryl was still holding her mask and Michael wore his on the top of his head.

Michael was the first to speak.

"You gotta put it on for it to work Sher."

Sheryl slowly pulled the mask over her head and strapped it to her face. Nothing happened for several seconds, but then she realized she'd been holding her breath. A few seconds later she had no choice but to try and breathe through the mask. When she inhaled, her vision immediately blurred and she felt very lightheaded. She stumbled and Michael caught her. She wanted to reach up and pull the mask off, but her arms refused to listen to her mind's orders. As she went limp in his arms, Michael set her down gently on the ground.

He put his face in front of hers and started talking, but she couldn't understand anything he was saying. She tried to scream for help, but her mouth wouldn't open either. She wanted the mask off.

Michael disappeared for a second and then reappeared. She saw him lean forward as if putting a kiss on her forehead, but felt nothing. She watched helplessly, her eyes the only part of her in her control, as he pulled her shirt up. He disappeared again and she began to panic. Internally, she screamed and tried to wake her body. She tried to get any part of her body to listen to her commands and move, but nothing responded.

Michael appeared a few seconds later and she calmed a little. He was now directly over her and she knew his body had to be straddling hers. She felt a sudden pain in her crotch and Michael started to pump up and down. Thankfully, the pain quickly subsided and was replaced by that same eerie sense of dullness. Through her bouncing vision, she felt the pounding as he thrust again and again. He continued for what seemed an eternity, but couldn't have been more than a couple of minutes, and then rolled off of her.

Jenny appeared and Sheryl felt hope rise for the first time that night. Jenny would help her. She would take the mask off and take her back home to safety. Jenny sat next to her and pulled the mask off. Sheryl tried to breath in the fresh air, but her lungs were doing their own thing and refused to listen to her request.

Michael put his head next to Jenny's and the fear returned. He reached up and removed the mask from his head. Jenny began kissing her on the lips and Sheryl watched as her hands stroked down her face and disappeared from her view. Jenny's kisses moved down her face and eventually moved too far for her to see. Sheryl had no idea what Jenny was doing to her until she briefly felt wetness in her crotch. Michael took his mask and put it over her face.

Sheryl's lungs suddenly worked and she jerked from her memories. There was no mask now and she took in breath after breath of clean air. The feeling began returning to her hands and feet. She was able to turn her head and see that nobody remained in her view. She tried to roll over to her stomach. A crippling pain in her crotch stopped her and she reached down to see what was causing the pain. Her fingers touched bare skin and wetness. Knowing she didn't want to see, but helpless to avoid it, she brought her hand back up to her face and looked in horror at the blood covering it.

Sheryl forced herself to roll over and get to her knees. Her clothes were strewn about her and she gathered them up. After several minutes she stood, on shaking legs, fully clothed. The sun was beginning to rise and she could see several other bodies scattered around the hangar.

Sheryl began the long walk home.

Hideaway

Hideaway

The sun bore relentlessly down on the lake and its capacity threatening crew of weekend seafarers. The summer had proven to be one of the hottest in recorded history and all of the public lakes were overcrowded. Businessmen turned ship's captains struggled to find open space as their limited steering experience was pushed to the limits. The weekend had already been witness to countless assaults and apologies as boats bumped, knocked, and rocked others. A ban on all water sports and a swimming distance restriction had been put into effect for the weekend for safety sake and the water patrol seemed more visible than ever.

All of these hassles and frustrations were taking their toll on two couples that'd planned on getting away from city life for the holiday weekend. Brian and Sherry, the owners of the boat, had extended an offer to Tyler and Victoria (call me Vicky) and the couple had happily accepted. The idea of escaping the shackles of city labor in favor of skiing or merely floating on the lake had been too enticing to be rejected and all the plans were made. Three hours earlier the four had been laughing at corny jokes on their way to the lake sixty miles from their homes. An hour later they'd laughed with some reserve at the extraordinary line of vehicles waiting to get into the dock area. The humor left completely when they crested the hill and saw the overloaded lake.

A brief discussion took place to decide if they should even pull the boat from the slip with such a crowd. The general consensus had been an agreement that the two-hour drive required them to at least try the lake. After a forty-minute trek to their favorite cove they dropped anchor and tried to enjoy the remainder of the day. Swimming in the cove proved impossible because of the proximity of the boats. The four's frustration increased with the temperature and it didn't take long to decide to try something else.

Brian trolled around the lake looking for a spot with more space, but his hopes sank as he passed each cove. The women decided to layout on the seats of the boat and soon fell asleep. Tyler decided to take the opportunity to view the scantily clad women on the other boats. They'd circled three quarters of the lake when Brian saw a narrow opening that withdrew into the surrounding woods. A 'Do Not Enter' sign attached to a chain hung across the opening along with a 'Shallow Water' sign.

"Hey Tye, you ever been down there." Brian pointed to the waterway.

Tyler followed Brian's finger and shook his head, "Probably just a runoff."

Brian looked at the boats surrounding him and saw no Water Patrol emblems. When he looked back to Tyler he was greeted with an evil grin of agreement. Brian shrugged his shoulders and Tyler nodded. Brian slowly drove the boat to the chain as Tyler crawled to the front.

"You better trim it before trying to go through man. I can't see anything, but better safe than sorry."

Brian nodded and raised the motor to a thirty-degree angle. Tyler raised the chain as they drove under it. Several people in the surrounding boats began to cheer and Brian faced them and gave a quick bow. They cleared the chain and drove out of sight of the lake as the cheers began to subside.

The waterway was about the width of two of Brian's boats and lined with large trees. Some of the trees hung over the water giving the group brief patches of shaded comfort. The roots of the closest trees grew out of the banks creating a somewhat ominous atmosphere.

"Tye. Keep a watch for anything up there would you?"

Tyler nodded and hung his head over the bow. The banks began to rise above the water creating mud cliffs. He watched as the water went from murky green to almost clear in a few hundred feet. He could see the bottom of the waterway and could even make out the few fish swimming in the area. He watched in awe as the fish swam under and around the boat. Brian's voice shook him from the hypnotic view.

"See anything yet?"

"You're not going to believe this, but I can see everything. This water is crystal clear and I don't see a rock anywhere."

"Ah, you were probably right then. When they make these runoff lanes they clear out all the debris, but I didn't know they chained them off. Must be too narrow for the novice captains." He took a second to laugh at his own joke and then continued. "I think I'm gonna just drop anchor here. Sound good?"

Tyler looked up the waterway and saw a clearing of trees about a hundred and fifty yards away.

"Wait a minute. There's a clearing up above. Why don't we go there and drop? It's a little wider and probably better swimming room."

"Good enough man. Just keep an eye out for trees and stuff in our way."

They pulled into the clearing and stared in amazement at the size of it. It was a circle about five times wider than their boat with an opening on either side. The sun shone through a break in the trees over their heads. Brian stopped the motor and dropped the anchor. The men woke the women and watched with pride as they took in the view. The women looked at each other, nodded, and then gave the men a sarcastic round of applause. The men ate the attention up.

Tyler spoke, "You should look into the water. It's so clear you can see the fish, the mud, everything."

The four of them made their way to the back of the boat and stood on the platform looking into the water. They could see the mud bottom of the waterway, but there were no fish.

Victoria looked at Tyler and raised her eyebrow. "I don't see any fish down there."

Sherry wrinkled her nose. "That's fine by me. I don't really like the idea of fish swimming around my feet anyway."

Victoria laughed and nodded her agreement.

Brian started laughing, "You are going in though, right?"

Sherry, still looking at the water, shrugged her shoulders.

Tyler moved to the back of the boat. "Well, you're not gonna keep me out of there. How about you Brian?"

Brian looked at Tyler and then jumped over the front of the boat. Tyler jumped in and they met at the side. They began swimming around the circle exploring their new find.

Meanwhile, Victoria sat on the inflatable raft she'd tied to the ladder while Sherry spread across the back of the boat, her feet dangling in the water. The noise of the busy lake was no more than a buzz in the background. The world they'd left behind had nearly slipped out of their minds.

In the middle of a conversation about the trials of work, Sherry caught a glimpse of motion in her peripheral vision. She turned her head, but could only see clear water and the mud below. As she turned back to Victoria, Brian yelled.

"Hey Tyler, check this thing out."

Sherry turned to see Brian swimming around a tree, but she couldn't see what he was looking at. Tyler swam over next to him and peered into the water.

"What is it?"

Brian shrugged his shoulders, "I don't know. You're the one that was born in the water."

"It looks kind of like an eel, but I've never seen one that fat. You think it's alive?"

Victoria noticed Sherry staring at the guys and asked, "What're they doing?"

Sherry turned back to Victoria and shrugged her shoulders. She looked back towards Brian and yelled, "What're you all looking at?"

Brian looked up and started to say something when Tyler screamed. Brian turned towards Tyler with a puzzled look on his face. Tyler jerked and then disappeared under the water.

Sherry stood on the back of the boat to get a better view as Victoria craned her neck. They watched in horror as the water around the tree changed from clear to red. Brian let out a scream of pain and disappeared under the water. Sherry yelled out his name and her voice echoed around the opening. The water became placid and silence filled her ears.

Brian's hand suddenly shot out of the water, wrapping around a large limb of the tree. He pulled the upper half of his body out of the water and Sherry could see pure fear on his face. His eyes scanned the water as his head shook back and forth. He looked at Sherry and began swimming towards her.

Sherry yelled, "Come on Brian. Faster, faster!"

He'd just cleared the stained water, now twice its original size, when he screamed out in pain and disappeared under the water again. Sherry watched as air bubbles began surfacing where he'd gone under. The water she'd been able to see through just seconds before was now cloudy and impenetrable. Blood bubbled to the surface forming another red circle that linked with the first.

Sherry found herself looking into a growing red mirror of water as Victoria sat motionless on her raft.

Sherry saw another blur of motion out of the corner of her eye and turned to see what it was. She saw nothing. She turned back to Victoria and saw a gray blur disappear beneath the raft.

"Victoria. Pull yourself to the boat."

Victoria was still looking at the spot where she'd last seen Brian. She didn't respond to Sherry's voice.

"Victoria!"

She turned and Sherry could see tears were forming in her eyes. Victoria's upper lip was quivering and Sherry knew she wasn't going to move. Sherry jumped down to the deck and reached for the rope connecting the boat to the raft. As her hand touched the rope, she saw another gray blur under the water. She grabbed the rope and began pulling the raft in.

Victoria let out a short screech when the raft first lurched forward. She saw what Sherry was doing and leaned forward to grab the rope. Her movement caused the raft to sway and she started to lose her balance. She grabbed the side and managed to regain control. She leaned forward again and managed to grab the rope. They both pulled and the raft covered a large distance. The raft was now within five feet of the boat and Sherry had her hand outstretched for Victoria to grab.

Victoria let go of the rope and reached towards her. Their fingertips brushed, but neither could gain a grasp and the raft drifted further away. Sherry pulled the rope again. Victoria's hand, still outstretched, got close enough for Sherry to grab. They locked their hands together and Sherry started to pull her to the deck. Sherry felt a smile start to spread across her face, but then looked to see Victoria's eyes widening. She followed her gaze and saw a growing gray blur directly under their hands.

Before either could react, an enormous head erupted from the water. In painful slow motion, Victoria watched as it opened its mouth showing large fanged teeth three rows deep. In one fluid motion, the mouth clamped shut and the head splashed back into the water.

Sherry stumbled backwards and rolled over the seat landing on the floor of the boat. Attempting to regain her balance, she put her hand against the floor and felt something odd. She looked down and saw she was still holding Victoria's hand in hers. Disgusted, she shook her arm and the hand flew into the water. Still shaking off the creepy feeling, she walked to the rear of the boat.

Victoria still sat on the edge of the raft, her arm extended as blood flowed from the end of the stump into the water. Her eyes were locked on the severed limb and not even Sherry's yelling could detract her from it.

Sherry watched helplessly as swarms of the gray blurs ran under and around the raft. The rope had fallen into the water and Sherry bent down to grab it. One of the blurs swam near the deck and she stood back up, afraid to reach into the water. A mass of gray now completely surrounded Veronica's raft and Sherry could do nothing more than watch.

The next events happened in an instant and Sherry was thankful for it. The raft deflated and Victoria began sinking into the water, still staring at her bleeding stump. A flurry of splashes encompassed the circumference of the ramp hiding the gory images from Sherry. When the splashing stopped there were no signs of Victoria or the raft.

Sherry felt nauseous and ran to the edge of the boat. Some of the gray blurs still swam around and she chose to vomit in the boat. She sat hunkered in the corner of the boat for several minutes trying to decide what to do. Eventually she gathered up the courage to stand up and look in the water again. The red was beginning to disappear and the original calmness was returning. There was no sign of the raft, her husband, or her two friends.

She walked to all edges of the boat and looked for the gray things, but found none. Beginning to regain her thoughts, Sherry made her way to the driver's seat and was relieved to see the key still in the ignition. As she turned the key she found herself thinking it wasn't going to start. This was all something from a bad horror movie and the boat was going to stall leaving her stranded here. However, the boat turned over and began rumbling under her feet. Water shot from the propeller of the motor and Sherry breathed a sigh of relief.

The boat still faced the other side of the opening and pointed directly to another waterway. Out of habit she wrapped the key string around her wrist. She began accelerating and guiding the boat towards the exit. A knock at the side of the boat startled her and she nearly let go of the steering wheel. Standing up and looking at the tiny wake behind her she saw several of the gray creatures moving towards her. There was another knock on the side of the boat and she decided she'd had enough. She shoved the accelerator and the boat lurched forward. With a quick glance behind her she was pleased to see a small pool of red seeping over her wake.

A grin crept across her face and she felt like giving the creatures the finger, but didn't want to take her hands off the wheel. She turned around just in time to see the branch that was hanging just at head level. The branch struck her in the head and caused her to stumble to the back of the boat and over the edge.

She felt cold water splash over her head and instinctively swam for the surface. She surfaced facing her boat and watched in awe as the engine died and it started to drift in the water. She looked at her wrist and saw the key still attached. Her fall had caused the key to come out of the ignition killing the motor, just as the salesman said it would. Remembering why she'd been running she began looking around for the gray creatures, but her vantage point and the waves prevented her from seeing anything. In a panic she began swimming towards the boat.

Resisting the urge to look behind her, she forced her eyes to lock on the back of the boat and the ladder. She'd covered more than half the distance when she heard a splash behind her. Without thinking, she turned to see what had caused the noise, but there was nothing there.

She turned back to the boat and was greeted by an open mouth of one of the creatures. She could see the rows of teeth were the same as the one that had attacked Victoria. A brief thought that this could be the same one passed through her mind. Sherry barely felt the teeth sink into her forehead and chin.

Shadow
Puppets

Shadow Puppets

Hugh Johnson looked around nervously as the detective on the other side of the table casually attempted to wear a path in the carpet. He looked around the tiny room for a clock, but found nothing on the walls. Glancing down at his watch he saw it was four in the afternoon. He'd walked into the station at nine in the morning, as soon as it became safe.

The first officer he ran into tried to dismiss him before hearing the story at all. When she turned to walk away he'd grabbed her out of panic. That simple motion caused a flurry of blue suited bodies to descend on Hugh. From that point, he'd been passed around various desks, telling his story (at least part of it) to each of them. Eventually, he'd ended up in this room with a Detective Jacob Sloan.

The detective slammed his hand on the metal table making Hugh jump in surprise. Hugh looked at Sloan and smiled. He'd always pictured police detectives as large, overbearing men like he saw in the movies. Sloan looked more like his vision of an accountant. He was tall, six foot two or three at least, but he couldn't weigh more than a hundred and sixty pounds. His wire rimmed glasses and balding head only emphasized the accountant image.

"What the hell are you smiling about?"

Sloan's voice sounded like an attempt at huskiness that fell just short of its mission. Hugh wanted to laugh at the attempt, but was just able to suppress it. Instead, he shook his head and removed the grin from his lips.

"That's better. Now, let's go over this again."

Hugh was tired of going over it. He'd been over it countless times and had no desire to do it again.

"Why?"

It was Sloan's turn to smile.

"Because what you're saying doesn't make any sense. Because I think you're feeding me a line of bullshit. But most of all because I want answers you're not giving me."

"No matter how many times I tell it, it's not going to change. I'm tired of..."

Hugh's voice trailed off and his body tensed as a shadow ran across the room, through him, and disappeared out the other side. He saw a person through the cracks in the blinds and relaxed again. Sloan watched the scene with a mixture of humor and pity.

"Well, we can sit in here all night if you want. I've got nowhere to go."

Hugh had regained his composure.

"Me either. I can stay."

Sloan stood and shrugged his shoulders in defeat.

"Have it your way Mr. Johnson. How about we save the taxpayers some money?"

Hugh gave a confused look, not sure where the detective was going with this. Sloan walked to the light switch and flicked the first switch to the off position. The row of lights behind Hugh extinguished in a fluorescent buzz of death. A light shadow appeared on the back wall.

"Looks like you've got yourself a little friend there Mr. Johnson."

Sloan pointed at the shadow and Hugh followed his finger. As his eyes landed on the vision, he tried to jump out of the chair, but the cuffs stopped him after only a few inches.

"Okay, okay. You win, I'll tell it again."

"I thought you'd see it my way."

"I first noticed the shadows a couple of months ago. Not that I hadn't seen a shadow before, but I noticed something weird about them a few months ago. I walked into my apartment and turned on the light, just like I'd done thousands of times before."

Sloan sat in his chair and looked over his notes as Hugh told his story one more time.

"I walked from the living room to the bedroom, my shadow following me all the way, just like countless times before. When I got to the bedroom I saw something out of the corner of my eye, but when I turned to look there was nothing there. I ignored it and turned on the bedroom light. I walked into the bathroom and thought I saw something again, but when I turned...nothing.

Once again, I wrote it off as my mind playing tricks on me and went on. I flicked the bathroom light on and cleaned up for the night. If you're curious about that, I shit, showered, and shaved. You should write that down.

Anyway, when I finished I turned the light off and walked back to the bedroom. I forgot something and walked back towards the bathroom. Just before I went through the doorway I noticed something funny. My shadow wasn't moving. For just a second it stayed still as I moved. I blinked and it was right where it should have been all along.

Naturally, that freaked me out. I tried to pass it off as an optical illusion or something similar, but my mind wouldn't let go. For the next couple of weeks, I started paying more attention to my shadow and kept finding problems with it. Sometimes I would move and it took too long to catch up.

Sometimes it didn't even try to catch up, it just walked away. Nobody else seemed to notice these things, but I was convinced there was something going on.

I set up video cameras and tried to catch the shadows off schedule. They never missed a beat when the camera was on. Those sons of bitches knew I was recording them and they made sure they got their jobs done. They almost had me convinced I was crazy several times, but then I'd catch them again.

I really didn't know what to think about it, but I never thought it would lead to where it did."

Hugh's voice cut off and he looked at the shadow behind him again. Sloan raised his head to see why he'd stopped.

"Mr. Johnson?"

No response.

Sloan reached behind and flicked another light switch off. The shadow on the wall crawled toward the ceiling. Hugh twisted in the chair and tried to jump out of it yet again. The chains tightened against his wrists and threw his body back into the chair. Sloan couldn't help but smile.

"I told you Mr. Johnson, we can do this all night long. Now, do you want to finish the story or do you want to keep playing this game?"

Obviously agitated, Hugh continually scanned the room as he shook his head.

"Then please continue."

Hugh tried to concentrate on telling his side of it, but the shadows were growing and he didn't trust them.

"I had just left the movie theater when I noticed my shadow was facing the wrong direction. Dozens of people walked by and not one of them noticed the difference, or if they did they didn't show it. Wondering if it were a play of the light, but knowing it wasn't, I turned down a practically empty side street. My shadow made the turn with me, but was still at the wrong angle. It just didn't match up with the lights and I knew it.

I stopped. My shadow stopped. I started to walk again. My shadow stayed in front of me. I couldn't believe how arrogant the bastard was being. I almost bumped into a man dressed in slacks and a sports jacket. He said something about watching where I was going. I turned to apologize, but he had already started to walk away. My shadow drifted past me and began following him even though I hadn't taken a step. I didn't know what else to do so I started following the shadow.

It stretched further and further away from me as the man walked faster. I decided to stand still because I thought the shadow would run out of length, but it never did. The man suddenly stopped and turned to face me. I thought he'd just caught on to the shadow, but instead he started to yell at me about following him.

I didn't know what he was talking about, I hadn't taken a single step. So I just stood there. Before I knew what was happening, my shadow reached out from the wall, grabbed him, and pulled him toward the wall. I think the man was too shocked to even scream initially. However, when it got him to the wall it began pulling him into it and that's when he found his voice.

He started screaming for me to help him, but I didn't know what to do. I just stood there and watched in awe as it ate him or absorbed him or whatever it did to him. Just a few seconds later there was nothing left of the man except his clothes. They dropped to the ground with a sickening thud and my shadow moved back to the right position. I walked over and picked up the clothes to see if there was anything left. There wasn't.

I dropped the clothes and began running. I tried to avoid all other people on the way home, but that's impossible in this city. I swear my shadow reached out several times, but it never got anybody else.

That was three nights ago. I stayed in my apartment with all the lights on for two days, but then one of my bulbs burnt out and the shadows found a way in. I waited until daybreak and then came in here.

That's all I know. I know it sounds ridiculous, but I swear it's the truth. Now, will you please turn the lights back on?"

Sloan finished writing on the pad and then looked back at Hugh.

"That man you're talking about was Keith Grayson. He'd gone out to pick something up at the store, but never made it back home. His girlfriend went looking for him, found the clothes, and called us. I hope your information will help us find Mr. Grayson safe and sound, but I need to do a few things before we let you out of here."

Hugh knew the cop was lying to him. He didn't believe him any more than the others had. With little other choice, Hugh decided he'd play the game with them.

"That's okay, but can you please turn back on the lights?"

Sloan ignored Hugh's request and walked out the door leaving the two switches off. Hugh heard a noise behind him and turned to find nothing but his shadow. He faced forward and tested the chains again. They were still very much secure. There was another noise behind him and he turned his head to find the source.

His voice temporarily forgotten, Hugh watched in silence as the shadows began joining, forming a giant shadow that encompassed the majority of the wall.

"Hey Cliff, I need psych down here. Got a crazy in room 3 that really needs their help."

"So I've heard. What's his story anyway?"

"I think he killed a guy over on Brighton a few nights ago, but he says the shadows did it."

"Wow. So the rumors are true."

A scream suddenly came from room number three. Sloan immediately pulled his pistol from the holster and ran to the door. He fumbled with his keys briefly, unlocked the door, and threw it open.

Leading with the barrel of the gun, Sloan entered the room and looked around. The man was nowhere to found, but half the room was cloaked in shadows. He reached out and turned on the two light switches, completely removing the shadows.

The room was almost completely empty. The only things in it were two chairs (one with handcuffs still attached), a table, and a pile of clothes sitting crumpled against the opposite wall.

DRAGON DAWN

Dragon Dawn

The cave opening stood gaping in front of the exhausted crew of six. The darkness seemed to taunt them, daring them to enter its domain. They were too tired to venture any further and decided to make camp in one of the trailers still remaining near the opening. The creature should sleep for another two or three days if their research proved to be correct. They should be safe.

Slayton chose a trailer wedged between two others in an attempt to hide their scent. He'd never been a hunter, but reports said they could smell humans and pick them out of buildings. Nobody had ever reported back after staying this close to a den either, but Slayton felt optimistic nonetheless. His crew ran through their drills flawlessly for weeks and they actually knew the layout (or the majority of it anyway) of this den.

Sharon had worked in the caves prior to the Dawn and was able to draw a rough sketch of the path. Killian took those sketches and drafted them into professional quality drawings. Slayton himself came up with the assault strategy.

Slayton decided to take both Sharon and Killian along. Sharon's knowledge of the landscape inside the caves assured her a position. The fact that Killian had been a ROTC member had sealed his place in the group. The other three (Phoster, Schelling, and Warner) were chosen strictly for their combat skills.

"Phoster. You take first guard. Schelling and Warner get some rest. Schelling will take second watch, Warner third. Two hour shifts and we leave at first daylight. Any questions?"

Slayton had been a high school football coach before and was used to barking out orders. The six took turns looking at each other, but nobody spoke.

"Good. Move out. Sharon. Killian. You two come over here. I want to go over the plans with you."

They climbed into the trailer and split into three groups. Schelling and Warner went to the far end of the trailer to get some rest. Slayton, Killian, and Sharon went to the middle and broke a fire stick to mull over the drawings. Phoster put the Safety-Eye on the side of the trailer, facing the cave, and closed the doors. The Safety-Eye had come out before the Dawn, but had been more popular with perverts in those days. It consisted of a small, magnetic base camera and a hand-held monitor. The camera transmitted radio signals to the monitor giving the user long distance capability, even through concrete.

The three went over the drawings for ten minutes before deciding they were still on the right path. The orange light from the fire stick was dimming and they agreed nothing else would be accomplished that night.

"You two better get some rest. It could be a long day tomorrow."

Sharon and Killian lay down on the cold metal floor, neither complained. Slayton walked over to Phoster's post.

"Anything yet?"

"I'm happy to say no, sir."

"Let's just hope it stays that way. And you don't have to call me sir you know?"

"Old habits and all that, sir."

"Fair enough Phoster. I'm going to lie down over there." He pointed toward the fire stick and the bodies of Sharon and Killian.

"Let me know if you need relief before the next shift."

"I'll be fine sir. Thank you."

Slayton nodded and went back to the middle of the trailer. It was going to be a short night and he knew it.

Killian was already snoring lightly and Sharon had her eyes closed. Slayton sat down behind Sharon, his back to Phoster, and stared at the fire stick. His thoughts were so focused he didn't even notice Sharon had edged towards him until she spoke, startling him.

"I can't sleep Slayton."

"I can't blame you. We're going to go into its den tomorrow and we have no idea what to expect. You have every right to be afraid."

There was a moment of silence before she spoke again.

"Do you remember the first time you saw one?"

The dim light still outlined his face and she could see him nod.

"What were you doing? How did you react? You don't have to tell me if you don't wanna, but I want to know."

"It's alright. I don't mind anymore. Maybe it'll bore you to sleep."

Twin orange grins grew on their mouths. Neither one noticed the other's.

"It was the Friday before Labor Day and I was driving home. Leslie and I were going to take the kids down to the Lake of the Ozarks that weekend

65

and I had left work a little early. My ploy didn't work though. Seems everyone else had the same idea and traffic was backed up for miles. I'm sure you've at least heard of the infamous traffic jams of the Grandview Triangle even if you never experienced them. Well, on holidays it got even worse.

I'd stopped just on the west side of the bridge that goes over Holmes. That damned glass business building was blinding me and I cursed myself for not remembering my sunglasses again. It was hot and I didn't have any Freon in my car so I had to rely on Mother Nature's air conditioning. Basically, that means that I could hear all the commotion and smell all the pollution very clearly.

You know, I drove that same path five days a week for eight years and nothing I imagined was even close. On stormy days I worried about twisters and lightning hitting my car. Can you believe that? I look back and wonder how I could have been so stupid. I guess we all were.

Anyway, I was sitting in the parking lot they call an interstate when I first saw it. A shadow passed over my car and I thought a cloud must be passing over, but the sky had been empty all day long and this shadow came out of nowhere. I looked up and had no idea what I was looking at. At first I thought it had to be a big bird that was closer than I thought, but I knew I couldn't be that far off. It just didn't make any sense.

This thing flew hundreds of feet over my car and I could still see every small detail on its body. The scales were shaped like guitar picks and overlapped each other. The coal black ones ran along both sides of the belly and blended with the gray ones that formed a line down its center. It had its huge wings, which were almost transparent with the sun as a background, outstretched allowing it to glide with ease across the sky. My first thoughts weren't of terror or fear, but were of awe at the beauty this thing displayed. How could such a large creature look so delicate and beautiful?

The car next to me ran into the car in front of him, obviously in as much awe as I was. If the traffic reporters had been able to make a report that night I'm sure there would have been hundreds of fender benders, but, as you know, nobody cared about fender benders after that day.

By now the thing was past the glass building and heading west at a good rate. I could see the tail swinging behind it and that's when I finally made the connection. It's a dragon. I used to play Dungeons & Dragons in college and it surprised me how long it took me to put the two together. I know some of the scientists are saying they're most likely some kind of dinosaur that made it, but I think that's pretty much bullshit. They're dragons and everybody knows it. That's why we called it Dragon Dawn.

The dragon was almost out of sight now. Some people actually got out of their cars to get a better look. Isn't that the stupidest thing you've ever heard?

I decided it was better to wait it out in my car. My father used to say, "Any fool who chases a tornado deserves to get killed by it. A smart man runs the other direction." He was quite the philosopher.

So these people are standing around on the interstate looking at the disappearing dragon and talking about what it must have been. That's when it turned. It didn't use a huge arc like you'd expect from something so large, instead it looked like it just stopped in mid air and turned 180 degrees. That's when the fear set in. I wanted to get out of there and get out fast, but there was nowhere for me to go. I was trapped in all directions by vehicles, most of which had no drivers in them. I had no choice but watch as it came back.

The traffic jam went on for about two miles behind me. I think it ended around the State Line overpass. At the tail end of the jam it opened its mouth. I couldn't actually see the mouth open, but I could see what followed all too clearly. I watched as a flame, wide enough at its base to encompass all four lanes of stopped traffic, came out of its mouth and began cooking everything in its path. I didn't know what to do. Should I stay in the car and take my chances or should I run to the ditch on the other side of the road?

Time made the choice for me. In the time it took me to question what action to take, the dragon's fire had made its way up to my place in line. I panicked and climbed into the back seat, toward the oncoming flame. I released the back seat and jumped into the trunk pulling the seat back up as the flames entered my windows. I could hear screams from all around and had to put my hands over my ears to deaden the noise. The heat was unbearable and I thought I'd be roasted alive. Most of the time I'm glad I was wrong.

I stayed in that damn trunk for close to two hours before I felt safe enough to come out. I flopped the seat back down, which was no small effort in itself, and climbed out the shattered window. The steering wheel drooped down to what remained of the front seat. The smell was horrendous and I noticed there were no flames burning inside the car. The heat had been so intense it burnt everything in a flash manner, not like a fire at all. If the interior had caught fire I probably would've suffocated from smoke inhalation. I walked around the car and all of the hinges had been melted preventing me from opening any doors or the trunk. I stood there in awe for several minutes looking at all the cars in the same state as mine. There were no traces of the people there at all. I know it sounds kind of funny, but I actually felt relieved they weren't there. I didn't have to look at the bodies of all those screaming voices.

I finally got my senses back and took in the whole picture. All of the buildings, including the big, glass business building, were demolished. The little trees and bushes they'd planted just last summer were gone. They weren't sitting there burning and they weren't turned into ash, they were just gone. The entire landscape looked black and lifeless. As I looked to the south and saw more black I thought of my family.

I ran as far as I could, then I walked, then I ran again. The whole time my mind kept putting horrible images in front of my eyes and I tried to block them out. I kept thinking, "This couldn't happen all over the city. It had to be an isolated problem!" I didn't know it was global until much, much later.

As you probably know there was nothing there when I got home. No wife, no kids, no house. It's that simple. I tried to lie to myself and say they got to shelter, but it wouldn't work. I knew better. I sat right where I thought my house should be and cried like a lost child until part of The Force showed up."

"That's pretty much my story in a nutshell. Whatdya think?"

Slayton turned to look at Sharon for the first time since he started talking. She'd fallen asleep.

"Guess it was that boring." Slayton smiled and went to the front of the trailer to check on Phoster.

Phoster turned and looked at him and Slayton thought he saw tears in his eyes. As he got closer the trace of tears disappeared and Slayton doubted he ever saw it in the first place. After a quick briefing, Slayton went to the rear of the truck and got Schelling to relieve Phoster for second shift. Slayton returned to the center and tried to catch a few winks before dawn. He only got a few.

A soft poking feeling on his shoulder interrupted Slayton's dreams of his wife and children. He awoke to the site of Schelling's face positioned just a few inches away from his nose. He figured it was time for his shift and started to get up. Schelling put his hand on Slayton's chest to keep him in place. His other hand came up and pointed to his eyes then to the Safety-Eye. Slayton rolled from his back to his stomach slowly, making sure not to hit his gear against the floor of the trailer. He pushed himself into a crouch and did the duck walk to the monitor.

At first Slayton only saw the darkness of the cave opening. Everything appeared normal and he was about to ask Schelling what he should be seeing when a slight motion caught his eye. He stared into the monitor trying to force his eyes to adapt to the lack of light. It didn't take long.

The dragon sat with its head poised in the cave opening. It didn't move much and Slayton knew that was no coincidence. He checked his watch and saw that he'd been asleep for about twenty minutes. He didn't want to wake the others unless it became necessary, but he didn't want to wait until they were in jeopardy either. He decided to wait it out. There wouldn't be much for them to do if it sensed them there anyway. The two of them watched for the next five minutes as the great wyrm cautiously crawled out of the cave. It began sniffing the air and the two men subconsciously stopped breathing. Slayton prepared to wake the others, but the dragon stretched its wings and flew off before he could bring himself to move.

They stood motionless for a few more seconds, partly out of caution, mostly out of awe, and then began waking the others. Quick preparations were made and they hurried out of the trailer and into the cave. The true journey began.

Using Killian's drawings and Sharon's memory the group moved through the caves many twists and turns searching for the lair. The maps showed detailed information about many of the known tunnels and passageways, but the location of the lair remained hidden. The crew moved as fast as they could knowing the dragon could return at any time. No surveillance had been able to find a pattern in their leaving or returning. Some in The Force wanted to wait until a pattern could be found, but the majority (Slayton included) thought they didn't have the time to wait for the discovery.

The inclusion of the two outsiders (Killian and Sharon) threw the usual deft and silent motions of the Strike Team off. Slayton felt much more vulnerable and wanted to get out of the cave as soon as possible. No Strike Team had ever come back when the dragon returned while they were still in the cave, The Force called them "live caves", and Slayton didn't think this crew would be the first to do so.

Slayton made the decision to leave the search and try again later. He felt the previous night's accommodations would not be safe again. The smell of the people in its cave would send it searching all around the area for them and they were too small a group to fight back. Not that it would do any good to fight anyway. Surveillance did prove that fact.

Warner carried the Safety-Eye monitor now and motioned to Slayton just as Slayton prepared to call the crew back. Slayton called a halt and went to look at the monitor. The dragon stood at the cave entrance sniffing the ground where they had entered. They were trapped.

"Shit! Everyone head down this tunnel and don't stop until I tell you to or until you hit a fucking wall. Go!"

Killian and Sharon ran into the tunnel first. Slayton and Phoster followed a few feet after. Warner and Schelling drew up the rear. Warner watched the monitor as the body of the dragon disappeared into the cave. They were blind again.

Killian searched the map for the tunnel they were in, hoping it would lead to a connection they could escape through.

"Sharon. What tunnel are we in?"

Sharon was running fast and couldn't read the map, which was bouncing in Killian's hands, so she searched her memory for it instead.

"I think we're in the Data Storage Auxiliary shaft. We just came off Main Shaft 3 and I think we're heading west."

"That puts us over a quarter mile in and we're heading to a dead end. Tell Slayton we need to turn around before it's too late."

Slayton had already caught up to them and heard what Killian had just said.

"I heard you myself. Quit looking at that damn map and keep running. It's already too late."

"If the scale of this map is anywhere near accurate, this tunnel is only about 250 yards long."

"Killian! Do you have any idea how far we've run already?"

"No. Why?"

"We've been running at a full sprint for nearly 2 minutes. That puts us about 150 to 175 yards into this tunnel. Do you see an end?"

Killian looked ahead, shining his light directly into the center of the tunnel, and saw no end in sight.

"I don't see anything! This light may not be bright enough for us to see it yet, but I know it's right up here."

"If you're right we're gonna have to try to make a stand at the end of it. I don't like it any more than you do, but that dragon is probably no more than a few hundred yards away from us now. You're welcome to go back, but the rest of us are heading straight ahead."

The idea of trying to maneuver his way through the caves alone, and with a dragon hunting him, didn't appeal to Killian and he put the map away.

The four kept running. Each of them thinking the end of the tunnel would appear with the next footstep and each giving a silent breath of relief when it didn't. Slayton decided to place the initial line of defense. He spoke to Schelling and Warner through the headset.

"Schelling. Warner. You two take posts about 5 seconds from your current position. This tunnel is supposed to end up here and we don't know where it really does yet. Set posts and move back a hundred feet every minute until I tell you otherwise. Understood?"

Schelling answered, "Affirmative Sir!"

Schelling ran to one side of the tunnel and Warner to the other. They both got into a crouched position and faced the opposite direction they'd been running. Their helmet lights shone into the blackness revealing nothing.

They waited for almost a full minute and were about to change positions when they heard it. The tunnel began to tremor and they could hear footsteps coming from an indiscernible position. In unison, the two lifted their weapons and waited for the beast to appear.

Slayton felt the tremors and knew they had to get somewhere soon or they'd be stuck out in the open. The end of the tunnel remained elusive and he knew they should be within feet of the closing wall. From the other end of the tunnel came a horrible screeching sound that reminded him of the old Godzilla movies. The unmistakable sound of automatic gunfire followed the screech telling him the dragon had turned the corner into this tunnel. The gunfire cut off suddenly and he felt his blood curdle. He fought the urge to turn around and run back to his men. His responsibility still remained with the destruction of the lair.

Phoster spoke bringing him back to the situation.

"I'll set up post here sir."

His voice was calm and resigned. He knew his duty and was giving Slayton an easy out. Slayton took it.

"All right Phoster. Good luck."

"Thank you, sir. I'll try to keep it off of you for a few seconds. Good luck."

Slayton nodded and Phoster stopped running. Slayton couldn't resist his urges this time and turned around to see Phoster walk to the tunnel wall. He quickly turned around and focused on Sharon and Killian.

Phoster's transmitter was still on and Slayton could hear him talking to himself.

"All right you mother, let's see how you take a couple of grenades up your ass."

There were no more team members to communicate with. Slayton switched off his headset and threw it against the wall. He heard a muffled explosion behind him and knew the dragon was there. Phoster couldn't be more than a few hundred feet behind their current location. He heard another muffled explosion. Phoster was gone.

He refused to turn around and see the creature that would end his life. Suddenly, Sharon and Killian, who'd been running side by side, disappeared from his view and he thought they'd fallen down. He discovered the true reason a second later when his foot failed to find the tunnel floor and he felt his body rolling down an incline. He rolled for several seconds before hitting semi-flat land again. He gathered his senses and jumped to his feet, weapon drawn. The light from his hat shone on the hill of rocks he'd just slid down. He saw the hill went up to a non-uniform hole that probably represented the tunnels former end. He saw Killian lying to the side of the hill of rocks. He moved his head and saw Sharon lying a few feet from where he stood. Slayton and Sharon had slid down the rock hill while Killian had missed the hill by a couple of feet and fallen the entire distance.

Slayton reached down and grabbed Sharon by the arm. She responded with a yelp of surprise, but stood up and took her place next to Slayton. A groan came from across the chamber and Slayton turned his light towards it. Killian was still alive and he began groaning. Slayton took a step towards Killian. A large, clawed foot came down on top of Killian instantly stopping the groaning. Slayton could hear the sickening sound of the body succumbing to the pressure of the foot. It sounded like the blood-fattened ticks he'd stepped on as a child.

The dragon began lowering the rest of its body into the chamber and Slayton took the opportunity to form a plan. He turned to Sharon.

"I've got explosives in my pack. I need you to go behind me and plug the two prongs into the plastics back there. You got it?"

Sharon nodded and moved behind him. The dragon lowered its head through the opening and stood directly across from them. Slayton had no idea how large the chamber was until he saw the dragon crouched in front of him. They'd found the lair. He felt Sharon open the straps on his pack and silently urged her on. He didn't know how long they had. The dragon lowered its head to his level and seemed to look him over. Sharon stopped. He wanted to urge her on, but didn't want to talk so he shrugged his shoulders trying to get her attention. It worked, but it also got the dragon's attention.

The dragon drew back quickly and Slayton could hear it inhaling. Sharon screamed and Slayton hoped she'd hooked both prongs up as he grabbed the trigger strapped to his leg. The dragon exhaled and a wall of flame descended from its mouth towards the two. Slayton pressed the trigger. He took little consolation in the fact that he'd been right: his crew wouldn't be the first to survive a live cave.

Little Goblins

Little Goblins

He could hear them outside his window, laughing and toying with him. They started off softly, but quickly grew into cacophonous ridicule. Hoping to deter them from his safety asylum, he'd extinguished all his lights long ago. Their gleeful cries carried through his closed, double pane windows mocking his attempts at obscurity.

A group of three or four, he couldn't tell for sure because many of their shrieks sounded alike, neared his home sending him into a panic. His heart beat so heavily in his chest he was sure they would hear it, and therefore him, and come barreling through the front door. His mind raced about so wildly and undirected that he didn't even notice his tired old body pressing itself into the recliner in an effort of concealment. The roar of the group reached a harrowing peak and held.

He could imagine their warped and disfigured bodies digging at his door with their sharpened claws. A board in one of the other rooms squeaked under the weight of an unknown visitor. He stopped breathing, waiting for the next sound or the inevitable end that loomed so near. The mob's voices began to subside, but he remained alert. The idea that one of them had somehow gained access to the inside of his house while the others lured him into comfort refused to leave his newly heightened mind. He listened, trying to draw more from his ears than he'd ever attempted before. Nothing.

He wanted to run to the window and throw the blinds, but the thought of seeing one of their faces looking back kept him seated. In his younger years he would have grabbed a baseball bat and opened the door willingly, silently hoping for one of the creatures to be there. Now was a different story. His sixty plus year old heart would likely not survive the shock and surprise of such an encounter. He didn't even have a bat in the house anymore. Blissful, and alarming at the same time, silence enveloped him.

Breathing returned without conscious effort as he imagined one of the little imps sneaking, under the cloak of silence of course, up behind his chair. It would wait for him to become complacent and then surprise him with a sudden swing of its razor nail. His throat would open and release a geyser, brief though it may be in his current state, of his life's blood onto his four hundred dollar faux Persian rug. The police would look at his withered old body lying comfortably against his chair and assume he'd done himself in. What did a single old man with no family or friends have to live for anyway? He'd asked himself that question many times since the death of his wife. A different kind of evil creature had taken her from him six years ago. Her evil creature had surfaced in her left breast and quickly consumed the rest of her even though the doctor had told them survival rates were growing every day. On a February morning, the survival rate took a severe beating and she'd been taken away from him.

He never thought there could be a worse way to die than the way he'd watched her slip away. Now he knew how naive he'd actually been at that time. She knew there was evil in her body and she knew, soon if not immediately, that it would overtake her. They were the same, her six years ago and him today, in that sense, but she had the benefit of pain killing and reality altering drugs. He had no such luxury. His demons were knocking on his door and when they got in (and they would get in) he would have to look them in the eye as they reached in and tore out his soul. Suddenly, the thought of slashing his own throat and saving himself the horror of looking into their lifeless faces looked pretty good. If he wasn't such a Christian he might have actually done it.

Light suddenly shone through the tiny window on his door and danced its way across the length of his living room wall casting ominous shadows along the way. They knew he was inside! Until that very moment he had held on to the possibility that they would just leave him alone thinking he'd left this dwelling and disappeared into the vast landscape beyond. It wasn't very farfetched considering he'd actually contemplated doing just that. In fact, had he known tonight would be the night he'd dreaded for many weeks now, he would have gotten in his car and just driven. But he hadn't known and now it was too late. His car sat motionless in his detached garage and the little beasts could be anywhere between his back door and the freedom of a not-so-late model Ford.

High pitched voices once again began their assault on the house next door. He could hear them chanting and then cackling their insidious laughter. He'd heard the first group of goblins actually get the widow Greenley nearly an hour ago. He'd been watching Matlock (thank God for reruns) when he heard gibberish coming from her front porch. The unenlightened widow had obviously opened the door without checking because nobody in their right mind would open their door to any of these things crawling along the streets tonight. Her screams sent him to the window to see the cause and that's when he saw the horde. Several small goblins sat on her porch leering toward her with their hands outstretched as she tried to fight them off. He wanted to run out his front door and across the short span of their yards to her rescue, but want is all he did. Instead, in a flurrying panic he dropped the shades of that window and ran through his house, as fast as a man his age can run, turning out the lights and closing the rest of the blinds. With the house in complete blackness, he'd run into the kitchen and grabbed the largest knife in the drawer. Twenty-three years in the same house came in useful when you were trying to move around in zero light.

The horror on her face played over and over in his mind as he tried to forget it. Would he have done the same thing if the widow Greenley had been his dearly departed wife? He hoped not, but his mind argued the point. He liked the widow and had actually grown quite fond of her over the last six months truth be known. So why would he have done anything more chivalrous or masculine had it been his wife? He probably wouldn't have.

The idea of him sitting idly by as a swarm of heathens took his wife into the depths of hell disturbed him more than the idea of being hunted by one in his house. What kind of husband, hell, what kind of human, would he be if he didn't at least try to do something? Not the kind he wanted to be, that was a definite. It was too late to help the poor widow, but maybe he could redeem himself a little in the eyes of his Lord.

He reached out and turned on the small lamp beside his chair. If they were going to come for him, he would face them with faith in his soul and pride in his heart.

A voice, very close this time, began speaking and he could actually understand some of its words. A reward for faith or just proof of how close they actually were? He wasn't sure, but he honed his ear on the voice anyway.

"The light's on. That means he's in there for sure. I told you he was hiding."

"I don't remember this light being on before."

"That's because he didn't want us to know he was in there. He thought he could just ignore us if he turned out the lights."

So he'd been right about their methods after all. They might have passed by his house all night if he hadn't turned on the light, but what about tomorrow or the next day. Still convinced he'd finally made the right decision, he stood up, knife in hand, and walked to the front door to await their confrontation. The demons had remained quiet since the exchange he'd understood. His palms began sweating, his pulse quickened, and his right hand gripped the knife tighter in anticipation.

The doorbell rang giving him the signal he'd been waiting for. He quickly threw open the door.

"Trick..."

He swung the knife at the dwarves in front of him. He saw an odd creature with a warped nose and half a mouth gasp in surprise and then in pain as the knife jabbed into its neck. With a speed even he thought himself incapable, he withdrew the knife and swung at the next goblin in line. This one had exposed bones and red eyes that remained fixed and lifeless even as the knife punctured its abdomen twice. He once again withdrew the knife and swung at the third and final creature in line. This one's scream of surprise was cut short as he inserted the knife into its throat. The tiny red, actually light red, maybe even pink, body stumbled and turned away exposing its wings to him. The wand in its hand fell to the ground with a familiar sound he couldn't quite place. The evil creature with angelic hair, funny how he'd missed the hair before, fell solidly next to the wand.

A scream erupted from the sidewalk at the end of his property and he looked up expecting to see another rush of goblins. What he saw was Mrs. Hannigan running with her arms extended and a look of pure shock on her face. For an instant, he believed she screamed out of relief and appreciation of his act of ridding their street of the filthy creatures, but then he understood. Jason and Justine Hannigan, identical twins on a normal day, and Jennifer Hannigan, usually her father's little princess, but a little fairy today, all lay dead in pools of their own blood. He was hardly aware of the widow Greenley running through her yard, just as he'd wished he'd been able to do, and looking at the gruesome sight displayed on his front lawn. He didn't even register her falling to her knees and then to the ground as her heart failed the same test he knew his would.

First Kiss

First Kiss

Brian Hobbs turned into his driveway wanting nothing more than to sit in front of his new television and watch the pseudo-live hockey game coming on in half an hour. Work had taken him longer than he'd expected almost causing him to be caught at the office all night. Another fifteen minutes of paperwork and he wouldn't have even risked the twenty minute drive home. But all of those concerns washed off him as he pulled off the freeway with the sun still ten, hell maybe even fifteen, degrees above the horizon. Now his only concern was whether the Slashers would be able to pull out of their three game losing streak.

He pressed the garage door opener button and waited for all of the environment checks to pass. When the machine decided there was a proper amount of sunlight, its internal clocks matched to a time within the threshold, and the body temperature of the driver of the vehicle was acceptable, the garage door quickly raised. Thoughts of the first line of garage attacks flashed through his mind, as they always did when he pressed the button. How those freaks figured out the frequency codes to override the original openers was beyond his capabilities to understand. But the images splashed on the television screen and newspapers had been enough for him to always accept this little delay with a sense of gratitude.

Trying to push those images out of his head, he began pulling into his stall - and quickly slammed on his brakes to avoid hitting Marilyn's little sports car - so much for a pleasant night at home with Kathy and the Slashers. It wasn't that he disliked Marilyn. In fact, he liked quite a few things about her. She had a good sense of humor and loved to flash that impish smile of hers all the time. She also liked to flash little glimpses of her ample breasts in his direction. Not to mention the way her deep red hair lying against her alabaster skin just drove him into a frenzy. That's pretty much where the positives ended. Based on the amount of time she spent at his house, she didn't seem to have a home of her own. That fact wouldn't be so bad, but every time she and Kathy got together, they discovered Brian was the source of all the world's problems. That seemed to be a high price to pay for a few quick views of a nice pair of breasts.

Silently cursing the women, he grabbed the remote, got out of the car, armed the vehicle, and walked into the garage. Instinctively, he took a safety look around, deemed it safe, and closed the garage door. He stood in the doorway and watched as the door closed amidst a flurry of ultraviolet light pulses and numerous mists of water. The gauge on the wall informed him he still had a month's worth of water left. Not bad, but with the rising cost of blessings they would have to be more conservative.

The heavy bolt on the silver door behind him disengaged; obviously confident he was who he claimed to be. Brian pushed it open and followed the giggles to the kitchen. At least they were laughing this time. He'd come home to find them in tears more than once and those nights were horrible.

He tried to sound cheery, but to himself he sounded fake. "Hey honey, what're you two schoolgirls up to tonight?"

The vocal ruse seemed to have succeeded. Kathy smiled as she spoke, "Nothing much. Marilyn was running a little late and I didn't want her out after dark so I told her to park on your side of the garage. We're going to have a little sleepover tonight."

It wasn't a question or even an attempt at Democracy, just a simple fact that she stated and he accepted.

Marilyn, dressed (sort of) in a half shirt and pink short-shorts, pushed her breasts in his direction causing his eyes to follow the bouncing balls. He quickly caught his fault and corrected it by rolling his eyes at his wife.

Marilyn didn't seem to notice, but her voice had that very impish tone he'd come to recognize. "Think you can handle two women in your house big boy?"

His mind tried to come back with a witty retort, but failed leaving him holding his mouth open like a fish on land. Pleased by her ability to throw him off his game, Marilyn turned and walked into the living room. Kathy gave him a quick eye roll and shake of her head before following.

Dammit! Why did he turn 16 every time that woman opened her mouth? It wasn't like he had a relationship at stake with her. There was just something about her that allured him beyond his normally high level of common sense.

Suddenly aware his mouth was still open, he closed it and took a quick inventory of the kitchen. The stove sat unused, the microwave read only the current time, and all of the countertops were immaculate. No dinner in sight. He would have to improvise, but he was good at that. Opening the refrigerator he saw the remaining three pieces of Wednesday's pizza and several cans of beer sticking out of the auto serving box. Two day old pizza had never hurt him and the beer would cure any stomach ailments anyway. He grabbed the entire box of pizza and two of the cans of beer.

Heading into the living room, he heard the women laughing again. Sure they were laughing at his fish imitation he'd unintentionally improvised moments earlier, he paused at the fringe of the doorway and took a deep breath before facing them.

The result turned out worse than he'd thought, the girls weren't laughing at him, they were laughing at one of the many drivel filled "chick" series that ruled the primetime arena. He now had less than ten minutes to get situated to catch the face off and the women had commandeered the television. The upstairs television had cable capabilities, but it was only a twenty-seven incher and no man could be expected to watch the Slashers on that small of a screen. Now was the time for his best bargaining abilities.

"So, are you girls going to be watching something at seven?"

Bargaining at its finest.

Kathy, without turning from the screen, responded, "Don't know. Why?"

Maybe it was time he took control, instead of trying to bargain he would dictate.

"Oh, I just need to know if I should watch the game upstairs or not."

Napoleon himself would have been proud of that demanding statement.

Kathy gave him a wave of the hand indicating she didn't have time to be bothered with his inane drivel. However, Marilyn came to his rescue this time. Not just a rarity, but unheard of in all the years he'd known her.

"Hockey? That's probably best watched on the big screen isn't it?" Without waiting for his response, she continued, "Hey Kath, why don't we go watch this upstairs and I can show you that new cream. I put some on my chest this morning, see?"

She was technically speaking to Kathy, but she leaned toward Brian. He could see all too clearly. Her alabaster skin looked as smooth as the ocean and disappeared into a shirt horizon he'd like to sail into. He wondered just how soft that skin would be if he reached out and touched it, even if just for a second.

"Sure, if it makes him stare at my chest like he is yours, I'll give it a shot."

Brian quickly shifted his glance to his wife's face. Even as his face flushed with embarrassment he visually tried to convince her of his innocence. The women bounced up the stairs sparing him even more awkwardness. He suddenly became aware of the pizza box and beer cans in his hands and remembered his original intent: the game.

He kicked off his work shoes, flopped onto the couch, and tuned to the game. Luck was with him after all, the national anthems were just being completed.

The next thirty-seven minutes went by almost instantly, the hollow box with two empty cans atop it were the only signs time had passed at all. Well, the only solid signs. Brian's bladder began to remind him that 24 ounces of beer exceeded his long term storage capacity. However, being the bladder of a hockey fan meant being considerate enough to wait until intermission to announce the call of nature. Good training.

Brian stood up and took a look around, suddenly aware of the emptiness of the bottom floor. The girls had actually left him alone for the entire period, another rarity. But hey, as long as the rarities kept working in his favor he had no intention of raising any flags.

The glory of an empty living room washed away as his bladder reminded him that it had held to its part of the deal, now he had to do his part. The downstairs bathroom was between the living room and the kitchen, perfect placement for those quick calls during the game. However, he needed to change out of his work clothes and get into proper hockey watching attire. The twenty minute intermission would give him plenty of time to change, take care of his bladder, and get back to the couch before the drop of the puck. Plus, he could gain a few points by checking up on the women - they loved that.

He began up the stairs two at a time, but quickly changed to one by one for comfort. Besides, he wasn't really in a rush. Why hurry back for the commercials?

There were two bathrooms upstairs. The guest bathroom in the main hallway and the master attached to the master bedroom. Going to the master meant walking through the women and possibly inviting them to destroy the rest of the evening. If he opted for the guest bathroom, he could go and check on them on his way back downstairs hopefully earning himself another wave of dismissal. This option was, by far, the better of the two possibilities. However, it would also require a bit of stealth on his part. Their bedroom door stood between him and the guest bathroom. He had to be careful not to draw too much attention or the entire plan could go south.

Trying to be as quiet as possible, he began softly stepping down the hallway. The bedroom door was mostly closed, but a large enough crack to expose him to the women existed. He paused at the door frame. Timing and silence were most crucial at this point. Inhaling, as quietly as possible of course, he took the entire width of the door in a single step and made it safely to the other side.

However, something had caught his eye as he'd passed the open portion of the door. The girls weren't sitting on the bed watching television as they typically did and the bathroom door had been open with the light off. Where had they gone without him noticing? They had to be in the house, darkness had fallen half an hour ago. Not even Marilyn was crazy enough to venture out at night with those things out there.

Curious, and a little worried, he stuck his face to the open door to get a better look around. The lights in the bedroom were lowered, but still bright enough to see everything clearly. From his position, he could see the television, currently showing some poor sap justifying his actions to two women (looks familiar enough), and the still empty end of the bed. Still leery of being torn from his game, he gently pushed the door enough to get his head through the opening.

The scene that revealed itself made him nervous, excited, and confused at the same time. Kathy and Marilyn were in the bed after all, but not watching television at all. From his newly gained vantage point, he could see Marilyn's nude body, every inch as pale and beautiful as the chest he'd seen earlier, set between Kathy's open legs. His wife's legs were tan and contrasted heavily against the white skin of her friend's. The scene looked like a snapshot of so many dreams he'd had after seeing Marilyn - sans himself of course.

Suddenly, a wave of deep red hair flew as Marilyn rose from between Kathy's legs. Her motion caused Brian to jerk in surprise closing the door on his head. He wanted to turn and run away, but seeing that red hair draped across the milky smooth skin kept him fixed. Arousal beat fear this time. He could hear Kathy moaning softly, but couldn't make out anything specific.

Marilyn, however, spoke softly, but very clearly. "I told you it'd feel good."

Confident he hadn't been spotted, he pushed the door off his head. Marilyn seemed to sense his presence at that time and whirled her head leaving Brian looking straight into her green eyes.

He'd been had and she was going to let out a scream so loud it would blow out his eardrum. Kathy would never forgive him for sneaking up on them and the end would begin.

But that's not what happened. Instead, Marilyn smiled that impish smile of hers and winked. With her hair covering half of her face as she gave him that look, she looked a bit like a little demon. A beautiful and sexy demon, but one full of evil thoughts. It turned him on even more.

However, fear won the battle this time and he quickly retreated out of the doorway and down the stairs - two at a time. Trying to appear as innocent as possible, he jumped back on the couch and tried to focus on the upcoming game. His heart pounded in his chest so loudly he could swear he heard it. His eyes kept looking at the stairs to see who would be coming to reprimand him, but nobody came. After a few minutes, he began to accept the fact that he'd gotten away with it. Maybe she hadn't seen him at all and the smile and wink were fabrications of his mind. Or, maybe those were signs that she wanted him to join them in the bed. God, the possibilities were as endless as they were exciting. What had he just passed up? What had he just risked? His bladder chirped in - why haven't you gone to the bathroom yet?

Alas, nature could not be ignored anymore regardless of the wonderfully beautiful images dancing in his head. He walked the short distance to the bathroom between the living room and kitchen and fulfilled his end of the bladder bargain.

When he came out of the bathroom, it was with a smile as his mind continuously played the upstairs scene. Kathy had never shown any bisexual tendencies before, at least not to him. How long had this little relationship been at a sexual level? Would he be allowed to join?

"Hey Bri. How's the game going?"

Her voice cut through the room like a knife. If he hadn't just used the bathroom, he would be throwing this pair of slacks in the trash.

Marilyn had somehow come downstairs while he was relieving himself. He really had to go, but there was still no way he'd spent more than five minutes in there. Now she sat fully clothed on the couch. How had she managed to dress and come down the stairs so quickly?

Once again, he did his fish imitation.

Marilyn was nowhere near as confused, "Are the Slashers winning? You know, they're my favorite team too. I just know Kath doesn't like sports so I try to keep that to myself."

He didn't know how to react. Here she was talking about hockey like nothing was different in the world. Maybe her acknowledgment of his presence had been all in his mind after all. He quickly thought of the game and the score.

"No, it's still zero-zero, but a good game. I think it's going to open up this period."

"Oh, so I haven't missed the face off?"

He was amazed, but at least his vocal chords were working again. "No, perfect timing actually."

He began walking to the recliner on the other side of the couch. The scene from earlier started to dissipate from his mind and he had almost convinced himself he'd been dreaming. There was just no other logical explanation for her actions or calmness.

"Hey, why don't you sit on the couch and explain a few things for me?"

Now his mind drifted to the possibilities of what could be about to happen. He'd never sat in the same room alone with the woman, let alone on the same couch in an otherwise empty room. Maybe he was still dreaming from earlier, or perhaps he'd died and this was his version of heaven. Either way, he wasn't going to let the opportunity pass by again.

Even with his mind convinced this was beyond reality, he sat at the opposite end of the couch leaving a full cushion between them. If this wasn't a dream, he would be welcoming an onslaught of jealousy and fighting if he sat any closer.

They sat in relative silence as the puck dropped and the second period began. Marilyn occasionally let out a sigh as the Slashers missed a prime scoring chance, but she asked no questions about the game. The longer this went on, the more Brian convinced himself he had been reading too much into her seating recommendation. He also determined he'd read too much into the scene upstairs. Things couldn't have been what he'd thought.

With thirteen minutes and twenty-seven seconds left in the second period and Brian's mind formally discharging all of the night's events, a large whack came from behind them. Marilyn jumped into Brian's arms and hid her face in his chest. For a second, he revelled in the feeling and wished for it never to end. But the sound had come from the large bay windows at the back of the living room. It could have been the wind. Another, heavier whack from the same location put doubt into that possibility and pushed her deeper into his chest. It had to be one of them.

Not wanting to let go of her, but needing to get things taken care of before there were problems Brian stood up.

"It's one of them isn't it?" Her voice trembled making her even more endearing.

Without attempting to, Brian's voice lowered, "I don't know, but better safe than sorry."

He sounded like the poor man's John Wayne from the classics. If he'd thrown in a "darling" at the end he'd have pegged it. Brian walked to the windows and pressed the button to open the exterior wood shutters. His senses seemed heightened and he could actually hear the whirring of the small motor. Wanting to step away until the shutters fully opened, but not wanting to lose the heroic stance he'd attained, he stared out at the blackness being slowly revealed. With every inch of night he expected to see one of them staring back at him. The shutters opened fully and the motor stopped whirring revealing nothing unusual. Brian breathed an internal sigh of relief.

"See, nothing to worry about."

As if in defiance of his words, a nightmarish body smacked into the large window. Brian jumped in surprise. Marilyn let out a small scream and buried her face into the couch. This wasn't the first time one of them had come banging on the windows in the middle of the night. However, something stopped Brian from pressing the ultraviolet flood light button quickly this time. Instead, he studied the grisly face that continued to press against the heavily reinforced glass.

It, he continued to refer to the creature as an it even though male features were very evident, had a face lacking any flesh color whatsoever. It looked more like the makeup application of a Kabuki artist. The skin was pulled taunt over the bones defining every skeletal structure normally hidden. It was grotesque and hideous, but so human at the same time. Its eyes were slate blue and stared at Brian with what looked like a pleading, of what he had no idea. The body of the creature was covered in a torn black t-shirt and tattered jeans. Its fingernails and toenails, clearly visable as it was barefoot, were long and unkempt.

These were the creatures that made people put holy water misters around every silver lined door. The ones that required everybody have a working set of ultraviolet floodlights for late night assaults. The reason all windows were made of four inch thick, reinforced glass. But most of all, they were the reason people feared the night and had to be prisoners in their own homes, or offices if they worked too late. They pretty much owned the night and all the policing and military interaction had done very little to stop that.

History classes had taught him about the rapid spread that had almost cost all the living their lives. He'd seen the biology movies that explained all their internal workings. In PE he learned all the lifesaving actions to use in a face to face confrontation, though he'd never had to use a one of them. And yet, he had no more understanding of this creature staring at him than he did of a nuclear fission.

The creatures tongue began rolling back and forth across the window leaving a disgusting saliva streak. Kathy would have his ass if he let that thing make a mess on her windows. Brian reached out and pressed the UV button. Night turned into day as the rear floodlights energized. The creature screamed, silent to Brian behind the thick windows, in pain and tried to flee. Before it could reach the edge of the patio it burst into flames and collapsed. Brian watched as the flames engulfed the tattered and torn clothes. Seconds later nothing but ash remained of the creature and its clothes. A soft wind came and took even that small reminder with it.

Brian released the button and closed the shutters. The creatures had become a little smarter over the years and rarely came near the houses, but something, probably starvation, brought the occasional straggler like this one. Nearly all of them suffered the same fate. Occasionally, they would react to the lights fast enough to get out of the perimeter. And rarely, ever so rarely thankfully, they would find a house with a weakness and be able to enter.

He went back to the couch and tried to comfort Marilyn. "It's okay, it's gone now. Things are back to normal."

She pulled her face out of the cushions and even though there were no tears, her voice sounded like crying. "Normal? How is this normal? Every time I think there is a normal, one of those...those...things come out of the woods and destroy everything. They're like animals. I can't even believe they were once human."

"I know, but one day things will change. You just have to have hope and live for the moment."

Her eyes burned their way into his sending his heart rate to the red line. There was a weakness, a vulnerability, in that look. She bit her lower lip, obviously deciding whether to speak or stay silent.

She chose to speak, "Do you really believe that? Live for the moment?"

He nodded. It wasn't just an answer to her question, but permission for her to do something else and he knew it. She leaned forward and pressed her pink lips to his. Fear had made them cold. So cold it nearly took his breath away, but then she opened her mouth and he filled her with his warmth. She pressed harder and harder against him until he fell back in submission. After what felt like an eternity of heaven, she pulled herself off of him.

Marilyn's eyes seemed to glow as she spoke, "Did you like that little show up there?"

Finally, she acknowledged he hadn't been dreaming or misread anything. He nodded, speechless once again in front of this beautiful woman.

"We can have that every night if you want. You, me, Kathy, and others can enjoy each other over and over again. Would you like that?"

Others? Kathy and Marilyn sounded like a good time, but who were these others? His mind raced for the right answer. He'd run from the doorway earlier and nearly missed the chance at this incredible feeling. Now she offered it, and more, to him. What other answer could there be? He nodded again.

She smiled, the now infamous impish grin, and spoke with a directed passion. "Safe from those wretched animals outside. They forgot who they once were, but we'll remember forever."

Her words sounded different to his ears now. What he'd thought was fear now sounded like resentment and anger. Before he could question her, she swung her head back throwing another wave of that beautiful red hair. He watched it settle on her shoulder in stunned amazement, a smile washed across his face.

She opened her mouth and licked her lips so sexually he knew he had to have her. Then he noticed the teeth to either side of her tongue, her canines, were growing. She withdrew her tongue as the teeth extended into fangs that touched her bottom lip. He wanted to push her off of him and run away, but she was fast. She lunged forward and buried the fangs into his neck. Brian felt pain as his skin tore and the teeth punctured his artery. And then, as quickly as it'd hurt, the pain disappeared. He could hear her sucking on his neck and he could feel her cold lips pressed against his skin, but there was nothing bad about it - the sensual kiss of a beautiful lady.

Marilyn moved her lips from his neck to his ear and whispered, "See, there's nothing to worry about. This feels good doesn't it?"

He searched for an argument as she moved back to his bleeding neck, but she was right. It felt great. He nodded.

When she raised her head he could feel the bleeding begin to subside. She sat back and looked straight into his eyes.

Her crimson lips moved, "You see, it is a disease, but it's a beautiful disease. We can live forever sharing the life blood of each other. Five of us produce enough blood to sustain the pack. We've been trained to fear it, but they were all wrong. Those are animals out there, the ones who take this gift and waste their lives. They are worthless and should be ridden of. But we're of a different type. You think those cretins would have figured a way to drive in the daylight? Or convince their friends to invite them into their house without going through the defenses? No. And that's why they'll all die of starvation, but we, you, me, Kathy, and others will live forever."

Living forever sounded pretty good to Brian.

Dark Ascent

Dark Ascent

How the hell did I get into this mess? I'm a white girl from a middle-income suburban family. How did it come to this? When did I go from sneaking cigarettes from the pantry to breaking into a tech. store holding a gun?

Mary Kristinson was crouched behind a large speaker display a few yards from the main entrance while Luke Brinston walked casually around the CD aisle. Luke was grabbing CD's, seemingly at random, and throwing them into the blue backpack Mary had lent him. The gun in Mary's hand was shaking uncontrollably while Luke's sat comfortably and motionless against his leg.

How can he be so calm? I've never even seen him with a gun, yet he carries it like he was born with it. He's always been calm, but we've never robbed a store before either. I just hope he hurries up so we can get the fuck out of here.

Seeming to notice she wasn't by his side any longer, Luke whisper yelled at her. "Come on! Get over here and start grabbing some of this shit!"

His voice did little to calm her and she remained crouched behind the speakers. Luke had talked her into coming along tonight (no small task in itself) and had even convinced her there was nothing wrong with it. When he spoke, everything that came out of his mouth seemed to make perfect sense. He was always right.

Now, crouching behind the speaker display holding a gun, Mary was wondering what she was thinking when she agreed to come along in the first place. This wasn't the first time he'd convinced her to do something she was against. In fact, he'd done it dozens of times before and everything had turned out just like he said. This time something felt different and she couldn't quite put her finger on it. Maybe it was the guns or the size of the store, but there was something eating away at Mary's stomach from the time she went through the service door five minutes ago.

Luke had a friend who worked for the store. The friend had agreed to tape the latch on the door so they could pull it open with little noise or effort. In exchange for his part, the friend wanted a third of the money and the collector's edition of the Die Hard trilogy on DVD. The deal was sealed and the friend, whom Mary had never met, had done his part just as planned.

The security system was a different story. The friend couldn't shut off the system because the manager always turned it on when she locked up for the evening and he didn't have the code. Mary had tried to call off the deal when Luke told her this, but Luke assured her that he had a plan for that too. The security system didn't have motion sensors because of a recurring rodent problem. Instead, the system was linked to all of the expensive items like the big screen televisions and the home theater systems. All they had to do was stick to the smaller stuff and they'd be fine. Mary agreed. It made perfect sense.

Mary looked at the gun in her hand and remembered his explanation for that too.

"We need to take some metal in case the manager comes back and we need to scare her to let us out. We won't use them. Nothing is worth that. I won't even load them. Will that make you happy?"

She'd nodded her agreement. What harm could an unloaded gun do anyway? Besides, if someone did show up they would need something to try before they could call the police. Once again, it all made perfect sense.

Luke had gone back to collecting more of the CD's and was moving as nonchalantly as if he were walking in his own home. Watching his calmness, Mary remembered the one time she had gone to his house to borrow Rob Zombie's latest CD. She'd thought it odd that he had her alone in his house and had never even tried to put the moves on her. Not that she would have fallen for his moves. She was sixteen and still a virgin and intended on staying that way until she was married.

Of course, she's always said she'd never rob a store or carry a gun before she'd met Luke either, but here she was doing both. Still crouching, she duck walked to the CD aisle. With every step she expected to hear the wail of a siren or the clang of an alarm, but none came. They'd been in the store for nearly ten minutes and there was no sign of the police. Mary thought the police could respond to any call within ten minutes so maybe Luke was right and there was nothing to worry about. She stood up.

"You finally calming down?" He gave her a smile that warmed her despite the fear and she nodded.

"Good. Start grabbing some of the DVD's over there and throw them into your pack. I'm almost done over here so I'll get you in a second. Okay?"

She nodded again and started to walk to the DVD aisle when she remembered something. She turned to Luke, who was already looking at the CD's again, and asked "He wanted the Die Hard trilogy right?"

"What? Who?"

"Your friend in the store. He wanted the Die Hard trilogy. Right?"

"Oh, yeah. Don't forget that. He'd fucking kill me if I forgot that."

She turned and began walking towards the DVD aisle again.

How do you forget about the guy who let you into the store in the first place? He's supposed to be his good friend and he just stared at me like I was an idiot. Maybe he's not so calm after all. Maybe it's all just a front for me. God, I love him.

Mary was grabbing the DVD's as fast as she could shovel them into the backpack when she caught movement out of the corner of her eye. Her body involuntarily jumped as all the possibilities ran through her mind. She turned her head toward the motion and saw Luke standing next to one of the big screen televisions in the home theater section. His hand disappeared behind the television.

What the hell is he doing? Don't tell me he's going to try to turn on the T.V. That'd be like calling the police and he's not that stupid. Besides, the power's off to everything in here anyway.

Luke withdrew his hand holding something in it. The parking lot lights shining through the front doors gave Mary enough light to see outlines of things pretty well, but she couldn't make out exactly what he was holding. It looked like a small cable of some kind.

The realization dawned on her and she yelled despite her fear.

"Luke! What the hell are you doing? That's the security cable! Put it down!"

Luke turned to her and she could make out a smile. Not the warming smile he'd offered just a few minutes ago, but a smile of evil intent and knowledge. She knew instantly that he planned on activating the alarm and calling the police - for what reason she had no idea.

Even as her mind put these pieces together her eyes saw him grab the wire with both hands and pull. Her ears were suddenly full of a sound that she'd never imagined. The clanging she'd envisioned while duck walking was nothing like this strange new sound. A breath later her vision was flooded with bright white light blinding her momentarily. The light disappeared leaving traces of millions of light creatures dancing on her eyelids. Before her eyes could adjust again to the dark, the bright white light again blinded her and she shut her eyes. It was a strobe.

Deaf and blind she began walking toward what she hoped would be the door they'd came in through. The backpack slipped from her fingers and she stumbled over it losing her balance. Her mind told her she was about to hit the ground and her body stiffened in response, but the impact never happened. She was suspended in mid-air by something. Squinting through tiny slits in her eyelids she saw blackness. The blinding light was gone, but the deafening sound was all too audible. She relaxed her eyelids a little more and her vision began adapting to the dark. Luke had prevented her from falling to the ground.

The same smile he'd given her as he pulled the security wire was sitting on his face as he helped her to her feet. As she looked around she realized she was between two large shelves of stereos and the strobe was being partially blocked. Her ears were getting used to the sound as well. Though she could still hear the alarm quite clearly, she was able to tone it out as Luke began speaking.

"Good thing I caught you. We can't have you knocking yourself out or you'll miss all the fun."

His voice was calm and relaxed, as usual. What was he talking about: fun? Mary's mind was reeling with questions, but her mouth failed to form any words. As though he could sense what she was thinking he continued to talk.

"We're just going to have a little fun with the manager. You see, she lives about three blocks from here and the police now refuse to respond to this alarm. Over the past few months they've had a lot of false signals and the store decided they don't want to pay for any more inquiries. The alarm goes straight to her house and she has to come check it out before calling the police."

Finally able to break her own silence Mary spoke.

"How do you know all this? Why are you doing this? Why?"

"I told you! It'll be fun. When she shows up you'll have to make a choice. Do you want her to call the cops or do you want to use the gun in your hand and get out of here? The choice is yours."

Mary looked down and was surprised to see she was still carrying the gun. She wasn't sure how she'd managed to keep her hold on it after she'd dropped the backpack, but it still remained in her hand.

"You said the gun's not loaded! What am I going to do with an unloaded gun? Goddamn it Luke! What the hell do you want me to do?"

The smile grew but remained sinister as he grabbed her head in his hands and pulled her face towards his. Nose to nose he spoke.

"I want you to do what you want to do. It's your choice. What're you going to do?"

The alarm suddenly went quiet and the building went into blackness again. Mary looked around and was surprised she could still see relatively well. Her eyes were beginning to react to the darkness when all of the overhead lights came on, momentarily blinding her again.

"It's time Mary! What are you going to do? Do you want to go to jail or do you want to take the easy way out? Make a choice and make it now!"

His voice had lost its calmness and he spoke in a hurried whisper. The tone made Mary nervous. Why had she agreed to come with the lunatic to begin with? Why was she even holding a gun, loaded or unloaded? She could feel a fog lifting from her mind as the thoughts became clearer and clearer.

The manager's voice pierced through the silence startling Mary.

"Are there any burglars in here? If there are, I'd just like to say a few words. Would you please shoot me? I'm getting so sick of coming down here every single night and turning off this damn alarm. At least if I get shot I can have a little vacation."

Mary turned to Luke, looking for guidance or some semblance of help. Luke was gone. He had somehow disappeared while she was thinking and now Mary was all alone, gun still in hand. Her mind was finally clear and her instincts yelled "Run!" so loudly she almost yelped in surprise. She began turning in circles, looking for the door they'd come through just minutes before. Her eyes landed on the red exit sign and she forced her legs to move her in that direction.

Only a few steps into her journey towards safety, the manager yelled down the aisle.

"Holy shit! Stop!"

Mary stopped and turned to look at the manager. She was wearing a pair of flannel pajamas and had a cellular phone in her hand.

"Please don't call the police. I haven't taken anything and my boyfriend talked me into it and I don't know where he is right now."

The last statement seemed to make the manager more nervous than before and Mary knew she'd made a mistake. The manager flipped the cellular phone open and dropped it as she tried to push the buttons. Mary's heart was beating so loud she could hear it vibrating in her ears. The manager bent down to pick up the phone, watching Mary the entire time.

"Please! Don't!" Mary pleaded with the manager, but her words didn't seem to affect the woman at all. She'd recovered the phone and was getting back up.

A tear formed in the corner of Mary's eye as she raised the gun. The manager had obviously not seen the gun before because her eyes bulged from her head now. Her fingers began furiously pushing buttons.

Mary made one last plea softly and almost to herself. "Please!" Mary felt the kick of the gun as she pulled the trigger. She watched as the manager was thrown backwards from the impact of the bullet. The smell of the spent cartridge wafted up to her nose and made her nauseous. Mary Kristinson dropped the gun that had just killed the manager.

A bright light appeared directly in front of her and Mary thought the alarm system had turned on again. However, this light was much brighter than the overhead fluorescent lights and the alarm strobe combined, but Mary wasn't blinded. She could see directly into the light and watched in amazement as it enlarged. A shadow appeared in the center of it and began growing as it came nearer. Mary didn't know why, but she felt no fear and was compelled to see who, or what, the shadow was.

Her curiosity was fulfilled within seconds as a man emerged from the light. The man was really quite ordinary: average height, average weight, and no distinguishing marks. Yet the man exuded beauty in a way that Mary had never felt. It took Mary a few seconds to place the image and when she did she began to understand. Images and memories began flooding her mind as the man began speaking. Mary saw a barn and a donkey.

"You have chosen the Dark Ascent and you are now responsible for carrying out of the destiny. Do you understand?"

Mary did understand some of it, but with so many questions she shook her head. Images still invaded her mind giving her brief glimpses into the responsibility of her actions. She saw three men in robes huddled around a newborn child.

"I am a messenger of God. I have been sent to inform you of your destiny. As the key to mankind, you have chosen the race's fate until the next coming. Two thousand years ago you chose the Path of Enlightenment and carried the child of Heaven. With the Dark Ascent you will carry the child of Hell. Nobody must know of this until He determines the time is right. Now go and let no one know what has transpired this night."

Everything was now clear and Mary knew what she'd done with her single act of murder. She saw an image of Christ on the crucifix and passed out.

Mary's trial took less than four days and the jury took less than three hours to come to the guilty verdict. Mary now awaits the birth of her child content to know that she, and her child, are safe from the world, behind the cell bars. She's not sure what she will name her child, but she has a feeling the name will come to her one night.

To The Ocean

To The Ocean

Bath time: the only real way to get away from it all. He stared down the hallway long before his mother left to run the water, anxiously awaiting his alone time. His eyes stared blankly as the television flashed frame after frame of mindless unreality, but his mind concentrated on the warm release of the water. He could feel the heat of their stares across the room and wanted to get away, but the clock said he still had five minutes left.

Mom always waited until the talk show ended before she would run his water. He didn't like the talk show, but it really didn't matter what he liked. She had a routine and rarely deviated from it. Sometimes, he wouldn't get a bath at all. He would watch the talk show end and wait for his mother to move, but she didn't. Usually on those nights, she would fall asleep on the couch and he would put himself to bed by lying on the floor and covering himself. The next morning he would wake to find her in the same position. Those nights were bad because he wouldn't get a bath, but they were also a little good because they were quiet.

The talk show ended and Mom stood up. She walked quietly past him and into the bathroom. Sometimes she would go into the bathroom, flush the toilet, and come right back out without running his water. He didn't like when she did that. He heard the water turn on and knew he would get his bath tonight.

She walked back and picked him up. Sometimes she would ask him if he was ready for a bath, but tonight she didn't speak at all. She took him into his room, undressed him, and carried him into the bathroom. He always got excited when he saw the water and he began to clap in anticipation. Mom grabbed his hands and held them together. She didn't like it when he got excited.

Mom lowered him into the tub and the inviting water. Tonight the water was hot and he pulled his feet away from it. She didn't notice, or she didn't care, and set him into it anyway. His bottom burned for a second and he rocked back and forth to get comfortable. Within a few seconds, he adapted to the extra heat. Mom walked out of the bathroom and left the door open. He wished she had closed it so he couldn't hear them as well, but she didn't seem to care about that either.

The yelling began almost instantly and he retreated into the comfort of the water. His eyes focused on the tiny waves that spread from the pouring stream to the edges of the tub in a never-ending cycle.

It hadn't always been this way. He remembered when Mom used to sit on the floor while he got his bath. She would talk to him and tell him all kinds of stories about the water. He liked those memories. When things got too loud, he would return to those days.

"Get me another beer while you're up." Dad's voice sounded loud and angry. His voice sounded that way a lot lately.

"You want a beer, you get off your unemployed ass and get it yourself." He could tell the difference between Mom and Dad's voice, but they sounded alike nonetheless.

"This unemployed ass puts food on the table and a roof over your head. Besides, last time I checked, your legs weren't broken. You can always get a job if you don't like it."

"I can't get a job that'll pay me more than it'd cost to put the baby in daycare and you know it."

"You should've thought of that before you quit taking the pill. The little bastard's been nothing but a money pit since he got here."

"If I'd known you were going to get fired I wouldn't have had him."

"I wouldn't have gotten fired if I didn't have to keep taking days off to take him to the doctor. Hell, I'd still have that job if it wasn't for him."

They yelled about a lot of things, but usually he would be mentioned before it was over. It seemed that both of their lives would be better if he wasn't around. He decided to remember one of the nights before the yelling started.

"Hey buddy. Are you ready to take a bath?" Mom's voice was soft and nice. It always made him smile just to hear it. He clapped his hands together anxiously and Mom laughed at him.

She turned to Dad. "Do you think he likes bath time or what?"

Dad smiled and slid closer to the two of them. Dad put his arm around him and gently kissed his forehead. "What's not to like? I know I'd like to get a bath from you."

Mom slapped (playfully, not like now) his hand and laughed. "You shouldn't talk like that in front of him."

"He's my boy, you know he's already thinking about it."

Mom picked him up and carried him to the bathroom. She sat him on the floor so she could turn on the water. After a few seconds of checking the water with her hand, she picked him up and took him to his bedroom. They would always go to his room to get undressed before the bath. He emerged wearing only a towel and more excited than ever. Mom wrapped her arms around him and began planting kisses all of his face and neck making him laugh.

She did that all the way from the bedroom to the bathroom. All the laughing hurt his stomach a little, but he loved it at the same time.

In the bathroom, she checked the water once more before putting him in. Once in the water, he began playing with his toys while Mom washed his hair. She sang a song about three men in a tub as she did it. Her voice sounded beautiful.

She let him play for several minutes after she'd washed him. He loved playing in the water without getting water poured over his face. For some reason, he could move better when he was in the water.

Eventually, Mom reached down and flipped a switch. The water slowly disappeared from around him telling him bath time was about to end. The first time he noticed the water going down he'd stared at the blackness of the drain in wonder. Even Mom's voice couldn't pull his attention away.

"That's the drain buddy. The water goes down there."

He kept staring at it trying to see the water moving, but it looked exactly the same.

"The water goes down the drain and into the sewer, but that's just the beginning of its journey. You see, all water wants to go to the ocean. So, we use the water when we take a bath or when I wash the dishes and then it goes into the sewer. When enough of it gets in the sewer, it begins making its way towards the river. All the sewers go the rivers and all the rivers go to the ocean. When the water reaches the ocean, it is surrounded by miles and miles of other water and it's finally happy."

The water no longer covered his legs and he could see it beginning to swirl around the drain. It finally looked like the water was moving. He looked at it and saw it really did look happy to be leaving the tub. He couldn't understand why anybody, even the water, would want to leave his house.

Now he understood. When the yelling started, he wanted to leave the house. He looked out the door to see what Mom and Dad were doing.

"Maybe if you'd spend less money on beer we could afford something better to eat." They were still yelling.

"Maybe if you'd spend less money on that kid's shit we could afford more for us."

"Babies are expensive. That's just the way it is."

They weren't throwing things or hitting each other yet, but he knew if he kept watching he would see it soon. He turned back to the water and saw it differently for the first time. The water was trapped in his tub and all it wanted to do was go to the ocean where it could be happy. He reached forward and flipped the drain switch to set it free.

It began racing down the drain and towards the ocean. He stared at it and wondered what it would feel like to be in the ocean. Miles and miles of water and no yelling or hitting. He liked that thought.

Suddenly, he saw something different in the water. He could see little balls inside the water, all of them touching each other to form one large piece. They looked back at him and began talking. "You can come with us. It's quiet in the ocean and everyone is happy."

That idea sounded good to him. All of the balls looked so happy as they swirled down the drain. He wanted to go with them and he wanted to go now.

"Come on. You have to come before we're all gone."

The water was going out faster than it was coming in and now it barely covered his fingers. It wouldn't be long until all of it disappeared. He reached for the drain. His finger pressed against the metal grate and he thought he'd be stuck in the house forever. As he watched, his finger began to get longer and thinner. It started to circle the drain and then disappeared into it. His hand followed the same pattern, then his arm and his body. He watched in painless awe as his entire body lengthened into a tiny sliver and poured itself down the drain.

He was on his way to the happy and quiet ocean at last.

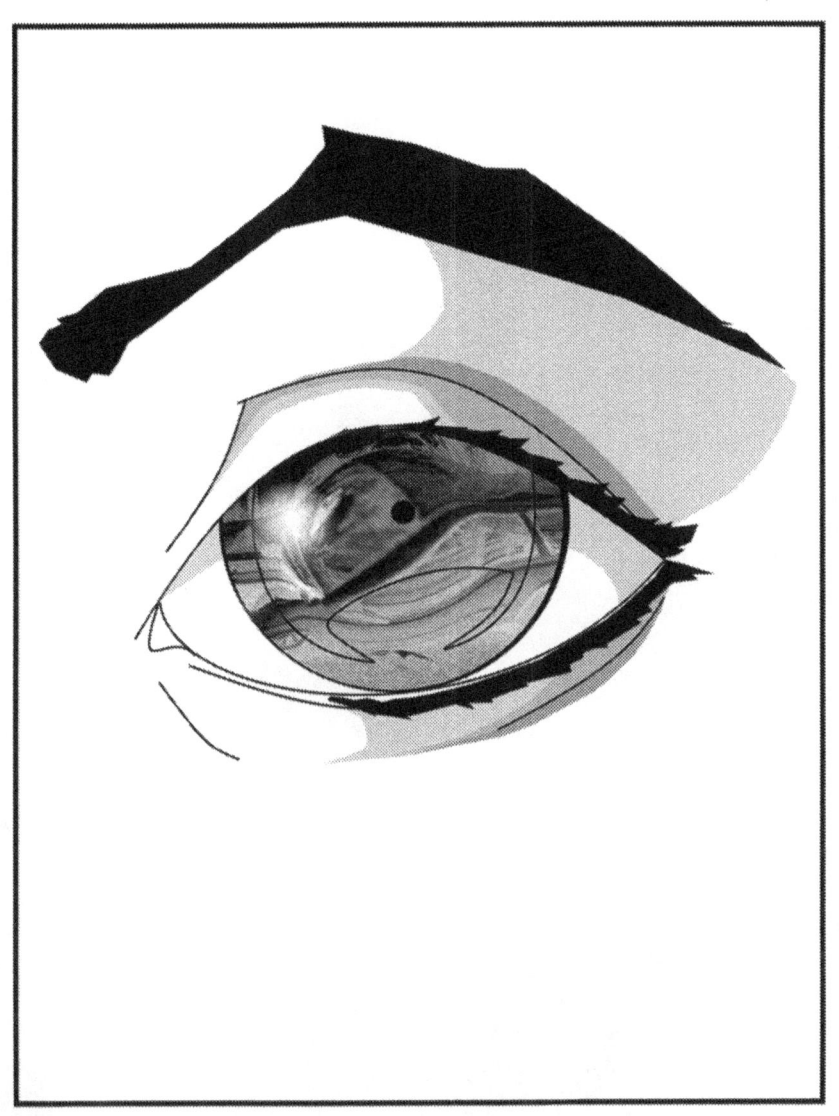

REFLECTIONS

Reflections

"It'll be okay son. We're going to do everything we can to make sure your parents are okay."

The voices had been pounding at him since the accident and he'd heard none of the words. His eyes were locked on the blue curtain that had been drawn to obscure his view. The blue of the curtain became a canvas on which his mind was painting his last visions of his family. He'd come in on the same type of wheeled bed that his mother and father (and Jayne of course) were brought in on. The difference was that they'd let him off his bed while the rest of his family was still tied down.

Now his mind was creating a scenario that he could not control and he was incapable of turning his head. He knew he had been bad and this was his punishment for acting that way. The blue canvas was being painted with images of mom strapped to the bed with the man doctor on her chest pushing frantically. The image was replaced with one of dad strapped to the bed with the big orange blocks on both sides of his head and the blood streaming across his face. That image was replaced with Jayne, poor motionless Jayne, strapped to the bed. The image of Jayne was different from the rest. There was very little activity around Jayne's bed. Only a single man pushing the bed, following the other members of the family with a pace that was causing him to fall further and further behind.

"Why don't you tell me your name honey?"

The woman's voice hadn't stopped since he'd been brought into this room, but he was unaware of a thing she'd said. The woman moved directly in front of him, mercifully blocking the still changing blue canvas. Her hands moved from her side to his shoulders and her body squared to his, putting him face to face with the woman. He blinked.

"You don't wanna look in there honey, talk to me instead. Okay?" The voice was warm and inviting. His eyes met the woman's for the first time. He nodded weakly.

"That's better. Now, can you tell me your name?"

Glancing back over her shoulder at the blue canvas, now empty, he answered. "Ryan Shulwater."

The woman smiled and her hands moved from his shoulders to his lap. Obviously happy that he'd answered her question she continued. "Do you know what happened Ryan?"

Taking another glance over the woman's shoulder at the empty blue canvas, he nodded.

"Good! We need you to sit here while we make sure you are okay. Your mom and dad are with the doctors right now and the doctors are trying to make them better. Do you understand?"

While nodding he asked the question he knew he didn't want to hear the answer to, "What about Jaynie?"

The smile vanished immediately from the woman's face answering the question without a word. Her face deceived her, but her words were that of a trained professional. "We don't know for sure yet honey. The doctors will have to let you know about that, but they're very busy right now."

Deciding to let the woman off the hook easily, he questioned no more. After all, it wasn't her fault; it was his. Apparently taking the reprieve as a sign, the woman walked away. He closed his eyes and let his mind drift.

"Ryan! Leave your sister alone and sit down!" Mom's voice.

"She started it! She took my book and now she won't give it back. Yell at her."

Jayne, smiling and still managing to stick her tongue out at him, "He wasn't reading it mom."

"Ryan! Sit down and put your belt back on. Now!"

The new van was big, much bigger than the station wagon they had just a month ago, and gave Ryan plenty of room to escape the long arm of his mom. He knew he could stay away from her long enough to get his book back and he really wanted that book. It was true he wasn't reading it, but he could want to read it at any time. What would he do if it wasn't there when he decided he did want to read it?

He jumped out of his seat and ran over to Jayne's. She shrieked as soon as his feet hit the floor. A high-pitched shriek that made him stop in fear for a split second. The split second was all that mom needed to reach back and grab him by the arm. Real fear set in.

Her face leaned toward him until their noses were touching and she spoke in a voice so quiet Ryan wasn't sure he was hearing her at all. "Sit your ass down and don't make me tell you again."

Ryan went back to his seat and glared at Jayne. He would get his book back.

"Hold on dear! We don't want you sleeping right now. Okay?"

He opened his eyes and he was back in the hospital with the same lady standing in front of him. Her smile had returned and her eyes were filled with a look of concern. He assumed she was worried about him going to sleep for some reason, but he wasn't asleep. He was remembering. His dad had told him once that when you remember things by seeing pictures in your head exactly as they had occurred, it's called reflecting. That's what he was doing, reflecting.

The door behind him opened and he looked to see who had come in. It was another doctor. The doctor smiled at Ryan then waved a hand at the lady who'd been talking to him. The woman patted his legs with her hands and told him that she'd be right back.

"Does he know how my mom and dad are?"

"I don't know honey." Her voice was soft and sympathetic. "Let me check and I'll let you know. Okay?"

Ryan nodded and turned back toward the blue canvas. The canvas began painting its horrible images again and he could not close his eyes or turn his head. The room was eerily quiet now and Ryan could almost hear the sirens again. Once again mercy was given to Ryan and the sirens were replaced with the conversation between the doctor who'd just walked in and the woman Ryan had been talking to. He couldn't understand what she was saying, but the man's words were very clear.

"The girl, Jayne I think, was dead before she got here. We just had to give a TOD on her. It doesn't look too good for either of the parents either. Guess nobody was wearing their seatbelts except for the boy over there."

There was a pause while the woman spoke, then the man continued, "I know. I guess some people don't learn until it's too late. It's sad really. I feel sorry for him the most. Losing your whole family at once."

Another pause, this one slightly longer than the last, then the man mumbled something else and walked out the same door he'd come through. The woman came back to Ryan and once again blocked his view of the blue canvas. She bent down so she could be at face level with him again.

"That doctor wasn't the one who worked on your sister or your mom and dad, but he said he'd check and let us know as soon as he can. You okay?"

Ryan picked up on the word 'worked' and knew that meant nobody was working on her right now. He knew she didn't mean to say it that way, but she'd said it nonetheless and he'd picked up on it. He paused.

"Hon, you okay?"

Ryan met her eyes and nodded weakly at her.

"Good. Are you gonna be okay if I leave you alone for a minute?"

Ryan continued nodding. The woman smiled, stood up, and walked out the door the doctor had gone through just a few minutes earlier. Ryan's vision became cloudy and distorted and he felt tears form in his eyes and roll down his cheeks. He squeezed his eyes tightly shut and reflected.

Jayne was reading the book, Mom was talking to Dad about which direction they should go, and Ryan was deciding when to make his move. She'd stolen his book when they first got into the van and Mom had taken her side, Ryan was pissed. He'd gone back to his seat, but had retained some of his pride by not buckling his seatbelt. The time was now and he was ready to make his move.

Ryan jumped from his seat and made it to Jayne's before anybody else in the van even noticed he'd moved. He grabbed the book from her and took flight back to his seat, but Jayne had a death grip on the book and he was stopped in his tracks. Mom's attention was diverted back to Jayne's seat and she turned as far as her seatbelt would allow. Dad never wore his seatbelt, but Mom always wore hers. Her arm reached toward Ryan, but Ryan had already seen her movements and moved further back into the van. Safely out of her reach, the battle for the book continued. Neither child willing to give up, neither child able to out pull the other.

"I told you to let her have the book Ryan! Now let go and get back into your seat."

Mom was taking Jayne's side again and he wasn't going to have any part of it. He knew he was already in trouble and had nothing to lose by holding on and making his point. He intensified his grip.

"I've had just about enough of this young man." With that statement Mom removed her seatbelt and stood up. Her body was in between her seat and Dad's seat and she was heading toward Ryan with a look of shear anger in her eyes.

For the first time, Dad's voice spoke above all others, "Dammit Ryan, give the book back and sit your ass down in that seat before I come back there and beat your ass. Do you hear me?"

Ryan heard, but he knew Dad couldn't get out of his seat while he was driving the van. He was safe from Dad, at least for now. Mom on the other hand was just about close enough to grab him and he knew there was nowhere else to go. Feeling he'd made his point, Ryan let go of the book and put his hands up like a felon in the lights of the police. Mom's hand shot out and grabbed Ryan by the wrist. He didn't resist. She pulled him toward the front of the van yanking him off his feet for a second. He reached for Jayne trying to get any kind of gratification for the trouble he was going through. He missed Jayne and ended up pushing her seatbelt release. Then Ryan was seated, unceremoniously, back into his seat.

"Put your seatbelt back on and I don't want to see you move another inch until we get to your grandmother's. Do you hear me?" Her speech sounded funny because she was talking through her teeth, but Ryan knew better than to laugh at her now. He nodded.

"Is this Ryan?" A new voice, a man's voice this time, stirred Ryan from his reflecting. He opened his eyes and saw the man. This man was not a doctor. He was wearing a suit, not the overcoats all the other people he'd seen today were wearing. The new man's voice was soft and pleasant, but it made Ryan nervous for a reason he didn't understand.

The woman he'd been talking to earlier was standing next to the new man and she nodded her answer to his question.

"Ryan, my name is Dr. Farthington." He was a doctor after all. Ryan was confused.

The man obviously saw Ryan's confusion and continued, "I'm not the kind of doctor that operates on people. I try to help people in other ways. Do you understand?"

Ryan didn't understand, but he didn't want to listen to this man any more than he had to. He nodded.

"Good. Do you know you were in a car accident with your family?"

Ryan nodded again.

"Well, I'm here to talk to you about that. Is that okay?"

Ryan didn't want to talk about it, but he wanted to know what this man knew about it. He nodded.

"Your mommy and daddy and sister were all hurt really badly in the accident."

Ryan hadn't called Mom and Dad mommy and daddy for years. This man thought he was a baby and Ryan almost started laughing at him, but he knew he shouldn't and was able to suppress it.

"The doctors worked really hard to make them alright again."

In a moment that made him ashamed almost as immediately as he thought he, Ryan hoped they were all hurt really badly. They had all picked on him and taken Jayne's side when he hadn't done anything wrong. He felt so badly for thinking that way, he almost cried right then.

"They did everything they could, but I'm afraid they couldn't make them better. Do you understand what I mean?"

Ryan understood, but couldn't bring himself to do anything. He was incapable of moving at all, he couldn't even nod.

"Ryan, I'm afraid they were all too hurt to be helped. We called your grandparents and they are on their way right now to pick you up. We wanted you to know before they showed up so you would understand why they were here. Do you have any questions?"

Now more ashamed than ever Ryan could not keep the tears back any longer. The tears began building and he couldn't take his mind away from that horrible thought he'd had just seconds before. How could he think that way? What kind of monster was he to have a thought like that? The tears could be held back no longer and Ryan began to cry uncontrollably. His eyes shut to spare him the sight of the two people looking at him; his mind began to reflect again.

"Put your seatbelt back on and I don't want to see you move another inch until we get to your grandmother's. Do you hear me?"

Ryan nodded.

Mom reached around and pulled the seatbelt across Ryan's chest until it clicked in the latch. She had probably been aware he didn't latch the belt last time and was going to make sure it was done. One more glare and she turned to go back to her seat.

Ryan's reflections began to move in slow motion.

Dad yells out, "What the fu…"

He is cut off in mid-sentence. Ryan cannot see what he is talking about, but he feels it a moment later. Ryan is jerked forward, but his seatbelt tightens around his shoulder and he is stopped. He is able to see Mom thrown forward, but his view of Dad is blocked by Dad's chair. Mom has nothing in her way to stop her and goes half the length of the van with her arms flailing. Her face, moments ago full of anger, now full of shock and horror.

Out of the corner of his eye he sees Jayne lurch forward and her seatbelt slide up from her waist. The latch he had accidentally undone earlier no longer held the belt in place. Unlike Mom, Jayne has a seat in front of her that prevents her from going too far forward. Her sweet, innocent, young face is distorted as it hits Mom's chair. Jayne's head went forward at an arc then was instantly straightened by an oddly audible snapping sound. Ryan's attention turns back to Mom.

Mom's path is no longer open; the dashboard hits her at the waist causing her to double over. The windshield stops the doubling over motion in mid-swing and her head crashes into the glass. Ryan blinks.

When his eyes open again he is able to see the aftermath all too clear. Jayne is sitting in an awkward position in front of her seat. She's not crying. Mom is lying in the short aisle between his seat and the dashboard. The windshield now bears an incredibly precise, blood-outlined indentation of her face. Dad is still blocked from his view by the seat, but Dad isn't moving or talking so he's not okay.

Ryan knows he did wrong and he knows he's going to be in trouble. Ryan waits for help.

Transitions

Transitions

The dreams had stopped several months ago, Steve Satherburg couldn't remember exactly how many months ago, but he did know they had quit. Everything had left at once: the pictures, the sounds, and worst of all, the control. Steve had always had excellent control over his dreams and suddenly he was helpless in them. His nights were filled with pitch-black visions. It hadn't bothered him too much at first. His days were busy and he didn't have much time to think about the loss of the dreams. Then the disease forced him into a hospital bed and he had plenty of time to think about it. In fact, he had too much time to think about it.

Steve had lived his entire life with the disease and was happy to have made it to sixty-three. Marfan syndrome ran in his bloodlines. He'd led a rather healthy and happy life and was willing to concede to the forces of nature.

Theresa, his oldest daughter, had offered to take him into her family's house, but he'd declined the offer not wanting to be a burden. His sons had offered later and he'd likewise declined their offers. After his wife died he'd become accustomed to living alone and understood the value of freedom. He was ready to accept death and wanted to make the transition to the afterlife with the dignity that he'd maintained for the better part of his life. Now he was in the hospital.

All of his children, and their children, were very reliable in their visits and did their best to comfort him. They followed proper hospital etiquette and made sure not to mention any bad news (it's not good for the patients you know). Steve was proud of his children and how they had grown up. Steve was proud of the life he'd lived.

I just wish I were still able to dream. I want to remember my Paula, before her body was ravaged by cancer. I want to walk with and talk to her in my dreams. I just wish I had my dreams to keep me company at night.

"Hi Grandpa!" Erick, Theresa's son, came running through his door and took his now familiar position next to Steve's bed.

"Hey there sonny boy. What're you doing here? Don't you have something better to do than sit next to an old man all day?"

"Dad, you know we're glad to be here." Theresa followed Erick's path carrying Paullette and a Quick Burger bag. Paullette had been born just after his wife died and Steve was silently happy Theresa had named her daughter after her.

As she got closer to his bed, she started shaking the bag. "Brought your favorite old man!"

"Still don't know where you learned to sneak stuff like you do, but I'm glad someone taught you." Steve winked at Theresa.

Theresa set the bag down on his lap and gave him a loving kiss on the forehead. She reclaimed her chair next to his bed.

"So, how are you doing today?"

"You know me honey, just glad to see you and Erick and Paullette. Stevie stopped by yesterday and you know what he brought? A salad! You know what salad does to a man my age?"

His voice was excited, but he was smiling. Stevie was his oldest son and had somehow grown into a fitness nut despite Steve's best efforts. Fitness nut or not, Steve loved him and was always happy to see him.

"You know he means well Dad. He was a fitness nut before you got sick and now he's totally crazy about it. I think he thinks he can keep it away from him by following all those health rules."

"I know, but the doctors have always told us diet doesn't mean a thing with this kind of disease. Unfortunately, it's inherited and it's all based on a roll of the dice. I've told him that time and time again. He just doesn't listen."

"I know Dad, but it's his way of dealing with it and being happy about his life. He's not like you, he thinks about this all of the time. This health stuff helps him put it out of his mind. There're also studies that say diet can help with some of the symptoms you know?"

Steve nodded his agreement and was more than happy to let the subject drop. Maybe there was something to that 'don't bring up bad news' thing after all.

Theresa and the kids stayed for an hour or so and then scampered off to run their lives as normal. He was always happy to see them, but he felt almost as good to see them leave. He didn't want them to change their lives just because he was in the hospital. He didn't want to be a burden.

It never failed to surprise him how exhausted he felt after his visitors left. He never thought talking could take so much out of him; it almost made him laugh.

Despite the fact that it was only six in the afternoon and despite the constant beeping next to his bed, Steve fell asleep. As he drifted into the formerly comforting darkness he made a silent wish.

Please let me dream of Paula.

Darkness. No color, no images, no Paula. Suddenly he heard something. It sounded like the beeping next to his bed, but deeper and not so intrusive. While the beeping next to his bed was annoying, this sound was almost comforting. His dreams now had sound, but there were still no images.

Steve awoke and looked at the clock against the wall opposite his bed. His vision was excellent for a sixty-three year old man with Marfan syndrome. He'd been lucky and hadn't acquired the common near-sightedness brought along by the disease. As he read the clock (6:23) he decided that was something else to be happy about: he still didn't need glasses. He'd slept for over 12 straight hours. That was a feat he hadn't been able to do for years. However, after more than 12 hours of rest he still didn't feel rested.

His dream had sound. Surely the visions would return soon. Steve wanted to go back to sleep, to see if the images would come back, if the sound would stay. It was too late, there was too much activity around for him to be able to go back to sleep. He was forced to wait.

Carl, Steve's youngest, arrived just before noon. He was carrying a Quick Burger bag in one hand and a cellular phone in the other. Carl set the bag on Steve's lap with a wink, kissed his father on the forehead, and sat down in the chair Theresa had sat in the day before.

"Alright, I gotta go. I'll call you in a couple of hours and we'll set up a meeting. Later."

Carl was the family's entrepreneur. In Steve's words, 'Carl owns a nifty computer company that does something or another on the Internet.' Carl showed up every two or three days, always talking on the phone when he walked in and always hanging up quickly when he sat down. Carl was the only one that knew anything about Steve's dreams, or lack of, as the case was.

"How you doing old man?"

"I'm breathing, got a Quick Burger, and have some sounds in my dreams now. Guess that's pretty good for someone my age."

"Sounds huh? That's an improvement. What kind of sounds?"

"Just a constant beeping type sound, not sure how to explain it, but it's definitely a sound. Maybe I'm not going crazy after all."

They smile in unison.

"Theresa and the kids stopped by yesterday. Snuck me in a burger too. I've trained you kids pretty well."

"Dad, I've told you before. We don't have to sneak them in, they don't care what you eat."

"So I'm not special? Thanks for bursting that bubble, boy."

Steve and Carl talked while eating the burgers from the bag. Conversation covered a variety of topics, including some bad news about some of Steve's friends. Carl never tried to shelter his Dad and Steve was glad for that, he needed the truth sometimes.

Carl left and Steve was true to form, he was exhausted again and it was only 1:45 in the afternoon. He decided not to fight the sleep. In truth, he was looking forward to sleeping to see what his dreams would hold.

Darkness. No images, no colors, but the sound came instantly. The same heavy beeping sound he'd heard before. He wasn't sure, but he thought he might be hearing other noises mixing in with the beeping. If they were there he could not discern what they were.

Over the next three months Steve's dreams continued with no vision. The other sounds he thought he heard began to split themselves into truly separate sounds. He was still unable to tell what these other sounds were, but he knew they were there for sure. Theresa, Stevie, Sandra, and Carl were very dutiful in their visits and continued to 'sneak' the Quick Burger bags in. Steve continued to fill Carl in on his dreams and how the sounds were becoming more discernable. Carl continued to read encouragement into these signs.

Steve's sleep patterns were beginning to worry him though. He was now sleeping at least twelve and as much as eighteen hours a night. The doctors and nurses didn't seem to be too concerned about it, but Steve didn't think it was right.

"Dad, the doctors say that it's normal for you to sleep more right now. They say between all the pain medicine and the nature of your illness it was bound to happen."

Steve had told Carl about his concerns and Carl had dutifully checked with the doctors for him. Steve was afraid to tell any of the other kids because of how they might have reacted, but he knew he could depend on Carl.

"That makes me feel better. Sorry if I worried you, but it was really starting to get to me."

"It's okay Dad, but why didn't you ask them yourself?"

"I don't want to sound like some whiney old man asking why I feel bad when I'm dying."

"Oh, knock it off old man. Nobody in their right mind thinks you are a whiner. Any luck figuring out what the noises in your dreams are?"

"Not yet, but I'm getting close. I don't know how I know, but I do."

any idea…thump…name is…thump…mumble…mumble…Tyler…thump…

"So they were voices huh? Could you make out what they were saying?" Carl had come on his now bi-daily visit, complete with Quick Burger bag.

"Yeah. Some of it anyway. They said 'his name is Tyler'. I woke up sweating and saying 'My name is Steve Satherburg.' Pretty weird huh?"

"Sounds pretty weird, but I've been thinking. You said you hear a beeping like this machine over here and now you're hearing voices. Maybe you're just not sleeping as heavily as you used too. Maybe you're hearing a muffled version of this machine and the nurses talking while you're asleep."

"I guess that makes sense."

It did make sense. It was so obvious he was surprised he didn't think of it before. He wasn't sleeping heavily, that explained the dreams and it explained why he was sleeping so much. Not surprising was that Carl, not the doctors, had been the one to figure it out.

"If I were you, I'd make sure they knew who you were old man. Don't want them giving you the wrong medication or something."

Steve looked up to see if Carl was being serious. Carl was smiling that wicked smile of his.

soothing…thump…make   it   easier…thump…Tyler…mumble…a   good parent…thump…mumble…hello…

Elevator music. Too loud.

Dad. Dad. Dad.

Steve's eyes opened and he looked in shock at Carl standing over him, shaking him.

"Dad? You okay?"

He was back in the hospital. There was no elevator music playing too loud and there were no nurses talking in his room.

"Dad?" Carl's voice sounded alarmed, but not panicked.

"Sorry Carl. I was just having another dream and you woke me up. Kind of startled me."

"Startled you? I came into your room and I see you twisting around in your bed saying 'My name is Steve Satherburg' over and over. I think I'm the one who should be startled."

"They were talking again and there was elevator music. Nobody is in my room and I don't hear the music now. What's wrong with me son?"

"Just a nightmare Dad. Don't worry about it. How long have you been asleep anyway?"

"Don't know. The days are all running together now and I can't tell when I'm asleep and when I'm awake. Tell the truth, I'm getting kind of nervous about this."

"Don't worry about it Dad. Probably just a case of the medicine and all the noise in this place. You know?"

Steve nodded. He really looked at Carl for the first time since he woke up. There was no Quick Burger bag and there was no cellular phone. Not that he could see anyway.

"Where's my burger? You didn't forget did you?"

Carl hesitated and his face tightened, "They say you can't have the burgers any more. Doctor says you need to start watching your diet a little closer. Nothing to worry about, just something the quacks here want to do."

That wasn't right. If the doctors told him not to bring anything in and they didn't have a good reason for it, Carl would have brought it anyway. There was something he wasn't telling Steve and Steve knew it. However, it wasn't Carl's fault and Steve didn't want to make him feel any worse than he probably already was.

"Well that sucks. Guess I'll just have to get used to eating the crap in here."

Carl's face loosened up and he became jovial again. Steve had made the right choice.

almost time to go…thump…are you ready?…thump…take care of Tyler…thump…see what the doctors think…thump…coming to an end…

Your father is quite ill…beep…not too much longer now…beep…spend as much time as you can…beep…as painless as possible…beep…make the tough choice…beep…I'm sorry

Are you okay?…thump…doctor's coming…thump…real soon now…thump

Dad…beep…he isn't answering…beep…Grandpa…beep…what's wrong with…beep…he going to die…beep…tell the doctor…beep…do it

Steve couldn't wake up. He could hear his children speaking to him, could hear the other voices and the noises, but he could not wake himself up. His vision was still filled with pitch-black nothingness. He began shouting, "My name is Steve Satherburg."

A tiny dot of bright white light was in the center of his vision. It began to grow very quickly. He tried to pull himself away from the light, to keep the light away. He wanted to return to the comforting blackness that plagued him for so many months. "My name is Steve Satherburg."

His struggles were in vain. He continued moving into the light and was blinded by its brightness. He could hear voices talking, different sounding voices than any he'd heard before. "My name is Steve Satherburg."

"My name is Steve…" He couldn't remember his last name.

"My name is…" He couldn't remember his name at all now.

"…" He couldn't remember what to say or how to say it.

"Congratulations! You have a healthy little baby boy. What's his name?"

"Tyler. We've always like Tyler."

poetry in motion

Poetry In Motion

The time was right. The conditions were perfect. It would, no, it must happen now. The man in the brown suit and the striped tie had made a mistake. It was probably a mistake he had made a hundred times before in his life and had never been made to pay for. Truth be known, it was a mistake that thousands of men and women made every day and most would never pay a price. The man in the brown suit and striped tie would not be one of those people. Today, he would pay.

Peyton came to this place every fifth day. His route varied very little week to week, but he did make sure to vary it enough not to be recognized by the repeaters. He'd never been caught before and he knew he never would be. The repeaters were mindless lemmings who did whatever the chasers told them to. It was nothing new in the ways of the world, nor was it something that was going to change. Peyton appreciated that and fed on the repeatability of the world. He was not a lemming and he was not a thought-crushing chaser, he was a selector.

His job, not the one used to pay the bills rather the one beset upon him by the higher being, was to select the persons who no longer deserved to walk the same land as he. That is why every weekday, without fail for 8 years, he would walk along the subway stations and make his selections. Some days, many more than not, there were no selections to be made and he returned home without fulfilling his duty. There was no anger on those days because he always knew the next day might be the same, and the next, but eventually he would find his selection.

Today his selection was the man in the brown suit and the striped tie. The man's mistake: standing too close to the tracks. His punishment: to be removed from Peyton's land. Most of Peyton's selection's mistakes seemed trivial when viewed alone, but Peyton knew the truth. It wasn't the single mistake he viewed that made them a viable selection; it was something much deeper. The viewed mistake was just a beacon sent to him so he could see the selections and be sure they were meant to be selected. He recognized the beacon, he'd seen it innumerable times before and would see it again he was sure.

The subway platform began shaking under his feet, another sign it was time, and Peyton began moving through the crowd. A crowd always gathered towards the edge of the platform a few minutes before the train arrived and there was always pushing and bouncing in that crowd. He would not be noticed any more than the woman in the gray business suit he just brushed past.

He was in position. The selection was in position. The repeaters were doing what they always did, repeating the same actions day after day. Peyton almost pitied them. They had no purpose, no goals (not true goals anyway), and no guidance. Peyton had them all. His purpose was to be a selector. His goal was to seek out the selected and rid his land of them. His guidance, which was pushing at him at this moment, was the higher being. He was alive.

The train's single light in the tunnel was now visible to Peyton and the sound of its metal wheels against the metal rails escalated. Three seconds left. It was down to a science now. His timing was always accurate and his execution flawless. Two. No increased heart rate, no sweaty palms, no rapid breathing. One. The lemming's heads turned in unison to the approaching train and Peyton gave a shove. Not the soft, inescapable shove resulting from a crowded subway platform, but a shove with a hidden strength and purpose.

The man in the bargain bin suit was pushed into the woman in the still business acceptable mini-skirt. She in turn stumbled into the woman in the stereotypical schoolteacher dress who fell into the young man wearing the shorts and listening to his Walkman. The young man was caught off guard and fell backwards into the man wearing the brown suit and the striped tie. The domino effect would have continued if there had been any more lemming dominoes to fall, but the line was done and the last domino could do nothing but fall.

The man in the brown suit and striped tie took on a look of surprise at first; the same look of surprise that usually accompanies a sudden loss of balance. Peyton could see directly into the man's face and could make out every line, every bump, and every twitch of the man's face. He always made a point to look at the selected's faces at that very moment. It was his gift from the higher being and he relished every microsecond of it.

The man in the brown suit and striped tie suddenly realized where he was going to fall and his faced changed. The look was now a look of sheer and utter fear. The look of a man who knows he is about to be struck by an object that will not even register the impact of his body on it. The look of a man who knows he is about to die.

The train was slowing down to make its stop at the station, but there was still plenty of speed for Peyton's purpose. The body wrapped in the brown suit and highlighted with the striped tie (it was no longer a man, the man had left immediately after the realization of imminent death) bounced off the front corner of the lead car and was propelled toward the trains departure tunnel. Again in unison, the repeater's heads turned to follow the body's ungraceful flight and even more ungraceful landing. Peyton's head mimicked the repeater's heads, partially to avoid drawing attention and partially out of need. Peyton knew nobody would pay any more attention to him if he didn't follow the body, but he still needed to rationalize it to himself.

The body bounced several times before coming to rest partially against one of the rails. Occasionally, Peyton would get lucky and the body would land on the infamous third rail and the entire flight would be finalized with a grotesquely beautiful fireworks show. Today it was not meant to be. The first time he had carried out the selection process Peyton was surprised at how little the repeater's reacted to the death of one of their own. Over the next 8 years his surprise had dulled, but refused to go away completely.

And there it was. The selection process had been carried out successfully once again and Peyton had been rewarded with the sight that none of the lemmings would ever know. His purpose and his goal satisfied and his worth reaffirmed. Today Peyton Lungston would be allowed to walk with the Gods if even for only a moment.

Four days later: different station, different lemmings, same purpose. The previous three days had yielded no repeaters worthy of being selected. The man in the brown suit and striped tie was the last and, of course, nobody had even contacted Peyton about the incident. He'd made his way up the stairs and back on the streets before the police had even arrived. It'd been perfect, as always.

The selected today was a man in blue jeans and a sports jacket. His mistake was missing the trashcan with his newspaper and failing to pick it up. The fact that the man didn't see the paper fall from the heaping trash can didn't waiver Peyton's belief in his selection. The selected wasn't going to make it as easy as the man in the brown suit and striped tie. This man stayed two rows of people from the ledge and was busy looking at all of the people around him instead of at his recently disposed paper. A challenge was presented and Peyton welcomed it. He'd been faced with challenges many times in the past and had always been led to the proper method, he knew this time would be no different. His mind opened and he awaited the knowledge of the higher being. It came.

Peyton moved into position by edging his way to the front of the line directly in front of the selected. The man's eyes were darting around the station looking at the hordes of people in front of him, away from the tracks; he didn't even notice Peyton moving in behind him. For his plan to work a diversion of some kind would be needed that he wouldn't be able to provide himself. He left the diversion to the higher being not questioning its possibility once. The diversion came as if on cue.

A woman and man were arguing, Peyton heard them when he first came into the station and had thought nothing of it at the time, and their argument had escalated into a fighting match. The repeaters followed the cue and turned their heads, in unison, towards the ensuing fight. Peyton's feet began feeling the vibrations of the oncoming subway train and he began counting. Five. Peyton turned to look for the familiar site of the single light on the front of the train. Four. The light appeared from around the corner. Three. Peyton bumps the man in the jeans and sport jacket forcing an involuntary pivot towards the tracks. Two. Peyton swings to the opposite direction of the involuntary pivot and moves up in the line to be even with the selected. One. The selected completes the pivot taking another involuntary movement towards the tracks to account for the area now being used by Peyton. Bingo. Peyton pushes the man in the blue jeans and sport jacket with one swift and calculated motion.

The selected body is launched directly in front of the slowing, but still deadly, subway train. The face of this selected body follows the exact same motions as all of the others, once again staying true to the title: repeaters. The now void body of the selected hits the front of the lead car and is bounced at an odd angle sending it back onto the platform and into a fray of people who had gathered to watch the fight between the man and woman. The people in the crowd who were fast enough, or fortunate enough, to avoid the body were spared being toppled and dropped unceremoniously to the floor. The lemmings turned in unison to the sound of screams and the thudding body giving Peyton another perfect path up the stairs and onto the streets. The higher being had given him everything he needed to complete the selection process and he had performed flawlessly. Peyton Lungston walked with the Gods once more.

Twelve days later: different station, different lemmings, same purpose. Not the longest period of no selections since he realized his purpose, but definitely in the top ten. Peyton was not upset, he was not nervous, he was not anxious, he was a man with a mission that does not change from one day to the next. His patience and dedication was about to pay off.

A woman wearing a blue business suit with a skirt had just shoved her way to the front of the line without saying a single word of courtesy. The sign had been given and Peyton began to get into position. As he walked to get to the proper position the method came to him from above in it's usual clarity and he knew exactly what to do. The repeater was selected, the method was defined, but the time was narrowing almost too quickly for the entire process to be right. Peyton increased his speed to account for the limited time. He'd run out of time several times before and had become quite aware of exactly how much time was needed versus that which was available. This looked like one of those times.

He'd been able to gently push his way to the front of the line four people down from the selected, but his time had just elapsed and he knew he'd have to call off the selection. He felt the vibration of the oncoming train under his feet and instinctively turned to look for the single light on the lead car. A woman's voice from behind him was loud enough to be heard above the rest of the crowd and the sound of the oncoming train. A single word drawing his attention, "Damn!" A glimmer of familiar silver caught his eye and he turned to see several coins rolling past him and towards the tracks. His selection cancelled he bent to retrieve the escaping coins before they dropped off the platform.

A sudden jolt to his bent waist caused Peyton to lose his balance and head uncontrollably towards the edge of the platform. Arms flailing helplessly to recover his balance, Peyton turned his head and saw the train about to arrive. Peyton felt his face form into the sickly familiar shapes and distorts against his will. He knew exactly what he looked like from the onlooker's eyes and understood what his selected repeaters felt like at this moment at the end of their lives. His feet searched feverishly for any kind of traction on the slick concrete floor. A moment later (his mind was not counting its well rehearsed times) his feet stuck to some gum on the floor and he was temporarily stopped. His body straightened from its crouched position and he stood straight and tall for a brief instant before his momentum carried him over the platform as the train went past him.

Peyton thought he'd be able to regain his balance and prevent himself from toppling off the platform. Then he fell. His body did not bounce off the lead train car as all of his selected bodies had; his body did exactly what he had tried to do for eight years. He felt his legs fall off the platform and reached for support against the slowing train. He knew his mistake even as he performed the action. His legs fell into the narrow opening between the train and the platform as his hands found grips on the first train car. He'd always laughed when he heard of people dying like this, all they had to do was stay calm and push off of the train as opposed to trying to regain their balance. Now he was doing the exact thing he laughed at them for.

Peyton Lungston knew his legs were being twisted in circles while everything above his waist continued facing the same direction even though he couldn't feel an ounce of pain. He knew there was no way of undoing the damage that was being done to him at this moment. He also knew he'd been pushed on purpose and though he'd live for several hours after the train stopped he'd not be able to tell the police who had pushed him. The police would listen to his story of being pushed and would patronize him until he died. The next day everybody who heard the story would say that he'd probably been standing too close to the edge and had fallen off on accident. He knew because this had been his goal on top of his primary goal. To execute such a perfectly timed action seemed an impossibility to him since he'd never once, in all eight of the years, been able to do it successfully. Even as the train slowed and he became aware of his own mortality he could not be sure the push had been timed for this purpose or if this had been just plain dumb luck. He'd die without knowing.

Sheryl Beckins watched the man in the gray dress slacks, light gray shirt, and horrible gray tie as he stumbled to gain his balance. She watched as he flailed his arms and turned to view the oncoming train that would be his vehicle out of her world. She watched his face fill with terror at the sight of the train coming and the knowledge of impending death. She watched as his feet stuck in the gum she'd dropped just minutes before. She watched as his face took on the brief, but very discernable, look of hope and salvation. She watched as the man realized the stop was momentary and that death truly was impending.

Sheryl Beckins watched as the man fell between the train and platform and she watched as his body was twisted an unknown number of times out of sight of all. Finally, she watched as the look of acceptance of his own death washed over his face and the look of fear was replaced with complacency. She watched all of this thinking to herself, "They never let me down. The repeaters have earned their name honestly and have lived up to it every single time. This repeater was no different than any of the others."

She'd been given the sign as she watched the rude man push his way to the front of the line never once looking at any of the people he was pushing to get there. She'd been told what to do and how to do it and she'd performed the task perfectly. As always.

www.ingramcontent.com/pod-product-compliance
Lightning Source LLC
Chambersburg PA
CBHW021115130626
46554CB00002B/705

9780615146690